Look out for more missions from

MEL BEEBY
AGENT ANGEL

www.agentangel.co.uk

going
for
gold

ANNIE DALTON

HarperCollins *Children's Books*

For my mother, who spent the two happiest
years of her life in Egypt.

A big thank you to Reuben for being such good company on
my Egyptian research trip, to Vivian French for suggesting
Cleopatra's time as a setting for Mel's tenth cosmic adventure
and to Jenny Pausacker for a useful talk that eventually led me
to Maia. Special mentions to Philip Ardagh and to Roger
Morkot from Exeter Museum, who both did their best to keep
me on the straight and narrow; any major slip-ups are all mine!

First published in Great Britain by HarperCollins *Children's Books* in 2007
HarperCollins *Children's Books* is a division of HarperCollins*Publishers* Ltd,
77–85 Fulham Palace Road, Hammersmith,
London, W6 8JB

The HarperCollins *Children's Books* website address is:
www.harpercollinschildrensbooks.co.uk

1 3 5 7 9 8 6 4 2

Text copyright © Annie Dalton 2007

ISBN-13: 978 0 00 716141 6
ISBN-10: 0 00 716141 7

The author and illustrator assert the moral right to be
identified as the author and illustrator of the work.

Printed and bound in England by
Clays Ltd, St Ives plc

CHAPTER ONE

Question: What are angels really made of?

Sorry, I know that sounds like a lead into a cheesy joke, the kind that makes me and my angel buddies snigger weakly into our hot chocolate when we've flown one too many missions. Like, *How many angel trainees does it take to change a lightbulb?** But I'm not joking. I'm really asking. You see, not so long ago I thought I knew the answer.

"Light, love and all things lovely. That's what angels are made of," I'd have said perkily, like an angel toddler reciting nursery rhymes. If you'd gone on to ask what angels were actually *for*, I would have had another snappy answer waiting on the tip of my tongue. "We are celestial troubleshooting agents working for a heavenly network of Light Agencies known as the Agency," I'd have reeled off confidently. "Our mission is to wake humans up and remind them what they're really on Earth to do. We comfort them, support them, watch over and protect them and, if absolutely necessary, we morph into a crack team of highly-trained divine warriors and get right into the mix to save them from the Powers of Darkness."

OK, so I might have said that with a few more 'urghs' and 'you knows'! The point is I absolutely KNEW where Mel Beeby, trainee angel, fitted into the Big Cosmic Picture. As an underachieving high school girl, I wasn't exactly a shining example to humankind, but as a surprise winner of a scholarship to the coolest school in the cosmos, a.k.a. the Angel Academy, I was now one of the Good Guys, no question.

That was before the Test.

If you think that sounds harmless, like some little spelling test – think again. You can *prepare* for a spelling test, you can memorise tricky words, and get someone to hear you spell them the night before. No one has a chance to prepare for the Test. This ancient angelic ordeal is shrouded in such total secrecy that a trainee angel has no way of knowing the Test even *exists*, until she comes tottering through to the other side with her self-esteem in tatters.

Anyway, how could you 'prepare' to lose a part of your soul – for a *minute*, let alone weeks or months?

I'm not sure if I ever used the word 'soul' in casual conversation when I was human, but just because I'm able to bandy it about doesn't mean I totally get what 'souls' are about, even now.

I do know my soul is a LOT more cosmic-minded than my everyday self. I know this because until recently I had pretty much twenty-four hour access to my own 'soul advice hotline', a.k.a. Helix my inner angel.

Helix and I didn't always see eye to eye, (she could be *très* opinionated for an inner angel, I have to say!) but her divine radar had got me out of some unbelievably dodgy cosmic situations. In fact, I was getting to rely on her to the point where I sometimes asked her advice *before* I got into trouble! I *know*!

Then one night – *nada*. Not even a tiny cheep from inner space.

It started after my first official angelic birthday.

Since angels are immortal, our birthdays are a bit different to the human kind. You still get a party and pressies, (this *is* Heaven!) but the main event is your angelic upgrade. In the long term your upgrade will hopefully make you a more insightful and more effective angel.

In the short term? You go completely bonkers.

No, babe, trust me on that, you do!

In an ideal Universe, you'd be given a few months to adjust to this new super-cosmic you. I got two hours max.

My headmaster Michael appeared (in the middle of my *birthday party* would you believe!) to tell me my three best friends from my old human comprehensive needed urgent cosmic support.

It was, without a doubt, the most absolutely harrowing mission I have ever been on. I came back totally haunted by my failure to help Sky Nolan, a girl who had once been my closest human friend. Just before I left, I found out she'd gone over to the Powers of Darkness – or her skanky boyfriend had – which, if you're a vulnerable thirteen-year-old girl, amounts to the same thing.

What got me was the Agency seemed to think my assignment was a big success. Michael and his assistant Sam were waiting for me in Arrivals all smiles. We finished my debriefing at about 2a.m., then they walked me out of the Agency building, put me in a staff limo and congratulated me all over again on my good work.

Michael popped his head through the window as I was sinking gratefully into my soft plushy seat. "You've been through a lot in a short time," he said, making the understatement of the year. "Your energy system might be a bit erratic for a while. I suggest you skip school tomorrow and catch up on some rest."

Our headmaster can be surprisingly human for an archangel, but it's unlike him to dish out advice. The Agency has a major bee in its bonnet about Free Will, which in practice seems to mean trainee angels are pretty much left to figure out the hard stuff all by ourselves.

But for once Michael was giving me a gentle warning. This crazy cosmic rollercoaster ride, otherwise known as my life, was about to get a LOT more bumpy.

At the time I just laughed.

"Yeah right!" We never get to take sickies at my school, not unless we're injured in the line of duty, and I'm talking hideous flesh wounds, not routine blood poisoning from getting too close to the Powers of Darkness.

By the time I reached the third landing on the long climb up to my poky little room in our school dorm, post-mission exhaustion was catching up fast. I actually had to lean against a wall, I felt so wobbly. That's how I came to notice the painting.

The Angel Academy has quite a collection of old fashioned oil paintings dotted around the school, dating back to the days when angels carried out their missions wearing pristine white robes. This particular painting showed a furious old-style angel banishing a hideous demon back to the Hell dimensions.

The picture of that calm confident angel doing what angels are supposed to do made me feel more ashamed than ever.

I dragged myself up the remaining flights of stairs to my room. Lola had pinned a note to my door in shimmery gold felt-tip.

"Wake me up as SOON as you get in and I'll run you a HUGE smelly bath and you can tell me ALL about it. Huge Love, Lollie."

Lola isn't just my best friend, she's my soulmate. We tell each other everything. Yet I still didn't feel able to tell her what had happened to my friend Sky. I can hardly bring myself to tell you now.

I let myself into my room, dumped my bag in the middle of the floor, fell on to my bed with all my clothes on and started to cry.

Sky Nolan came from what celeb watchers in magazines love to describe as a 'troubled' background. Not that Sky was a celeb (though she could be a right little diva sometimes), but once she trusted you, she was a real laugh – and she had *such* huge dreams.

One time my mates all stayed over at my place and we were playing that game, *if you could win a night out with a Big Name, who would it be?* Everyone named a certain drop-dead-gorgeous singer from a local hip-hop band, except Sky who picked Cleopatra, Queen of the Nile!

We're like, "*ARE YOU CRAZY?* Why would you CHOOSE to go out with a dead Egyptian queen!"

"I'm betting you never saw that movie where she has herself delivered to Caesar in a carpet!" she snickered.

We all gawped at her as if she'd sprouted a second head.

"Why did she do that exactly?" I asked politely.

"Caesar's soldiers had taken over her palace," she explained. "It was the only way she could get back in and regain control of her kingdom."

"Oh totally," Jax agreed, nodding wisely. "I've used the old carpet trick myself. Works every time!"

"Well, *I* think she had style," Sky said defensively. "You could learn a LOT from a chick like that!"

I could see her going all huffy. On a bad day, Sky could have totally sulked for England. I rushed to smooth things over. "Aren't you all forgetting something?" I teased my friends. "Sky's a smooth operator. She'd sweet-talk Cleopatra into inviting us back to her place, wouldn't you, babe?"

All my mates screamed with laughter.

"A royal sleepover!" Sky giggled. "How cool would that be! We could rollerblade through her palace and try on her golden shoes!"

Back in my room at the Angel Academy I could feel new tears welling up and trickling back into my hair. Can you imagine how it feels to see your fragile best friend walk away into the dark, perhaps forever – because YOU didn't save her?

At times like these, my inner angel normally comes online to comfort me, reminding me of the Big Cosmic Picture.

Remember that little thing called cosmic timing, sweetie? Helix might have said that night. *Maybe the Universe still has plans for you guys? Maybe you'll meet Sky again in some totally different time or place, and get a second chance?*

She could well have said something like this. Maybe she did? Maybe she was beaming fabulous cosmic advice at me all night long and I just wasn't able to pick up?

I don't pretend to know the technical ins and outs of Inner Angel Loss, so I'll try to stick to the facts. Without her divine radar system, a trainee angel is flying blind. When this angel girl, (OK, me) is a total *mess* of emotions left over from a traumatic mission, *plus* HUMONGOUSLY unstable from her recent upgrade, she is downright dangerous, to herself and to the Universe.

I didn't know any of this. I hadn't even noticed Helix had gone walkabout, which was disturbing in itself. I could cry when I think how much I didn't know.

I was so dumb. It never once occurred to me that a tiny speck of that ugly Darkness we were all so busy fighting was secretly hiding inside me, had been there ever since I started my angelic training, just biding its time.

And now all this shimmery birthday Light energy was starting to flood my system, flushing out any lurking cosmic impurities like some kind of celestial Draino.

I'm making it sound like it was really bad timing; the Test and the upgrade coming so close together, my divine radar on the fritz. In fact it happened this way for a reason. That's what the Test IS: the Powers of Light flushing the Powers of Darkness out of hiding so they can really duke it out. In the open.

With no inner angel for support, you're forced to find out what you're *really* made of. Now you're all alone in a dangerous Universe, can you face your own ugly demons and survive? Have you got the guts to dig deep and go for gold? Are you truly an angel? Or was that just a beautiful dream?

Like I said, I didn't know any of this, I just knew I felt completely rubbish.

Scrunching myself up into a ball of pure misery, I fell into one of those black sleeps that is so much more tiring than being awake. Even in my sleep I felt totally alone – final proof that the most dangerous part of my training was about to begin.

Chapter Two

Just three hours later I was like a completely new angel girl!

I woke up to find celestial sun beams dancing on my eyelashes, feeling happy, rested and ready for anything.

Cosmic upgrades will do that; drop you down into the depths one minute, send you soaring high as a kite the next. You'd think I'd make the connection, but no; I just yawned and stretched, mildly surprised that I could still hear the same spellbinding sounds I'd heard inside my dreams.

It sounds like diamonds, I thought drowsily, if diamonds could sing. I giggled at myself. "Singing diamonds, that'll be it, Mel!"

Very gradually it dawned on me that these crystal clear sounds were real. They appeared to be coming from right outside my window. I padded across the room and pulled up the blind.

Three little birds gazed back bright-eyed from my windowsill. Next second their tiny chests puffed out, their beaks opened wide, and the Mystery of the Singing Diamonds was solved!

I heard excited knocking at my door and ran to let Lola in.

"Lollie, the weirdest thing—!"

We ducked as a flock of tiny humming birds swooped in through my open window, wings whirring at the speed of light.

"Lala-lalala!" my friend sang out teasingly. "Melanie's had her upgrade!"

"My birthday was weeks ago," I objected. "I was using my new powers the whole time I was away."

"Ah, that was just a tiny taster, *carita*! Upgrades are a major deal."

I felt a flicker of alarm. "Major in what way?"

"Like it takes *months* to get back to normal. Meanwhile, you're walking around with a seriously spangly aura – that's what attracted your little bird dudes!"

 16

As we were talking my little bird dudes were happily redecorating my room with tasteful greenish-white splatters.

Lola got a good look at me for the first time. "Boo, *please* tell me you didn't sleep in those crusty clothes?" She pointed me sternly towards my bathroom. "Soap, hot water!" she commanded. "Then I'm taking you out to breakfast!"

My soulmate and I are so in tune, no one ever believes we grew up in totally different time periods, not to mention on completely different continents! Lola was born in a vibey third world country, one hundred years in my future, and I lived in London's gritty inner city one hundred years in Lola's past.

The spooky thing is I *always* knew I was going to meet her.

I didn't know that we'd meet up at angel school, or that one day we'd be watching each other's backs in the never-ending war between the Light and Dark agencies, but I knew she was out there, and I TOTALLY knew we were going to get together. Meanwhile, in a drastically different cosmic post code, Lola was feeling exactly the same about me!

Twenty minutes later my soulmate and I were hurrying through the buzzy streets of Ambrosia (the boho studenty area of the Heavenly City) on our way to Guru. Mo's cafe is really pretty much our second home.

Mo himself was placing fresh flowers on our usual table as we rocked up. "Good timing!" he beamed. "Can I interest you girls in the breakfast special?"

We didn't have time, so Mo went smoothly to plan B. He was back in minutes with two blueberry shakes (ideal for cosmic stress, if you believe Mo) and a huge plate of freshly-made peach and passion fruit muffins.

I waited till Mo left to serve some customers.

"Lollie, I feel really dumb asking this, but why don't I remember birds serenading you after *your* upgrade?"

"Maybe because it wasn't birds with me, it was butterflies." Lola saw my face and giggled. "They didn't serenade me, silly! They were just, like, magnetically attracted to me. Once a crowd of tiny blue butterflies literally followed me into class."

I shook my head. "I can't have been here. I definitely would have remembered that."

"No, you were," she said calmly. "I think it's one of those things that probably slips under your radar, until it happens to you."

Lola's explanation made me feel a teensy bit paranoid. What else might I be missing, simply because it wasn't on my radar yet?

"Unless you're a bird or a butterfly – or a preschooler!" Lola added, starting on another muffin. "They notice *everything*!"

"Obi does for sure!"

Obi is a preschooler at the angel nursery where I help out. It's wrong to have favourites, but if I did, Obi would be a serious contender!

"Talking of sweet angel boys," Lola smirked, "Reuben said to tell you 'Hi!'"

"Why can't he say 'hi' himself?" I felt like I hadn't seen my boy buddy for aeons.

"He signed up for a field trip while you were away to – where was it again? Atlantis, I think it was."

"Is that even *real*?"

Some angel boys at the next table were watching us. They seemed amazed that Lola and I could consume huge quantities of muffins, *and* chat like we were speed dating, all at the same time!

What can I say? We're girls. We had no choice! We had urgent catching up to do. While I'd been away, Lola had been rehearsing for a concert she had coming up. My friend literally has an angelic singing voice – one thing we *don't* share, I'm sorry to say. Obviously Lola wanted to hear all about my emotional reunion with my mum and my little sister on Earth.

"Oh, how did things work out with Sky?" Lola remembered suddenly. "You sounded so worried last time you called."

I thought I was going to fall apart right there in Guru.

Lola quickly put her hand over mine. "Is it too soon to talk about it?"

"A bit," I gulped, fighting tears.

Heavenly hip-hop music exploded from my friend's jacket. She pulled out her phone, beaming when she saw the caller ID. "Do you mind, babe?"

"Course not. Say 'hi' to your bad boy from me."

A LOT of water has flowed under the bridge since I first met Brice, Lola's cosmic drop-out boyfriend, in wartime London. When the school took him back on probation, I didn't trust that angel boy an INCH! I'm happy to tell you he has since proved me totally and utterly wrong.

As it happened, we'd both been in my old human neighbourhood working on different, but, as it turned out, totally cosmically-related missions. Brice was going to be there for another few days, tying up loose ends.

To give the lovebirds some privacy, I checked my mobile for text messages. Lola and I seem fated to end up with identical phones! Lollie had acquired this new Omni-Era XL22 while I was away. The Agency lent me the same model for my mission and to my delight, (the Omni-Era XL has zillions of spangly functions!) Sam said I could keep it.

After Lola finished her call, we quickly drained our smoothies and set off back to school.

"I meant to tell you, Amber had her upgrade while you were away." Lola was half-giggling before she'd even got her story out. "She's telling everyone she's only wearing pure white from now on. Says it'll make it easier to radiate cosmic light throughout the Universe!"

My jaw dropped. "White all over? Even her shoes?"

"She doesn't believe in shoes these days either!" Lola explained. "They block the light flow, according to Amber. She's all bare feet and tinkly ankle bracelets now! I'd keep out of her way, actually, she's looking for angel girls to join a bizarre group she's starting, called Sisters of Light!"

I couldn't help laughing. Amber was going to be soo embarrassed when her cosmic after-effects finally wore off!

"Hi, Melanie!" said a clear little voice.

I glanced down to see a small angel boy beaming up at me. It was Obi, the cutest four year old in Heaven. To my surprise, he seemed to be all alone.

"Where's Miss Dove, sweetie?"

"Well, aksherly," he said calmly, "she's at school teaching the other angel kids." He slid a sticky hand into mine.

"You should be in school too Obi," I told him. "What are you doing wandering around all by yourself?"

"I wanted to see your sparkles! They woke me up aksherly!" he added with a delighted giggle.

I was astounded. "You *heard* my aura – in your *sleep*?"

My sentence ended in a squeak as an unusually large blackbird landed on my shoulder in a rush of feathers. It gave my ear a friendly nibble.

"Cut that out." I told it, giggling.

The air was suddenly full of whirring wings, as birds of all colours and sizes came swooping down to admire my 'sparkles'.

The little angel boy's eyes were shining with awe. "The birds *love* you Melanie!" he breathed.

Quite without any warning, I felt myself whoosh through to a higher level of existence. In that dazzling instant I understood that EVERYTHING in the Universe loved me! Not just birds and cute little angel boys but germs and stars and blades of grass. Most wonderful of all, I loved them all right back!

I tilted my head back, letting the sunlight fall on my face like kisses. The air smelled of lilacs. Every leaf on every tree glowed like a vivid green jewel.

I felt so – pure and – yes, POWERFUL. Like, I just had to think the right thoughts and wild flowers would come sprouting up through the pavement at my feet!

Lola was watching with a resigned expression. She gave a deep sigh. "Oh man! Your upgrade is kicking in *big time*!"

CHAPTER THREE

I truly don't know where Lola gets her patience. Somehow she successfully coaxed her babbling best friend (me again!) to school next day. We had almost reached our classroom when a teeny gold butterfly flitted past leaving joyful energy trails like shimmery ribbons in the air.

Suddenly I had to be as free as that butterfly, or I was going to DIE.

I backed away from the door. "Sorry, I can't go in."

"Of course you can, sweetie," she said, in the gentle-but-firm voice she'd been using ever since my upgrade kicked in. "Anyway, I don't think Mr Allbright will be too happy if you bunk off."

"I don't care," I objected. "I mean, why do angels even *need* to go to school? Don't laugh, Lollie, I'm serious! Do you have the slightest idea how much cosmic wisdom there is in ONE tiny flower?"

My soulmate sensibly didn't even bother to reply. "Come on, little Bambi!" she grinned. "You can talk to the tiny flowers after school. Tell you what, we'll go to the gym later so you can burn off some of this surplus energy."

I let her march me into school, but I was fuming all through Mr Allbright's lesson. Lola was acting like I was going through some little *phase*. It didn't occur to her this might be the new super-cosmic Mel Beeby! My 'surplus energy' was my precious birthday gift from the cosmic angels, which they were trusting me to share with the whole Universe.

My brilliant idea hit me so fast I saw stars!

To our classmates' astonishment, I threw my arms round Lola. "I didn't mean to be a diva! You were just trying to help! I see that now."

Lola gently-but-firmly pushed me back into my seat. "Sweetie, Mr Allbright is trying to teach a maths class," she whispered.

Everyone was hiding their smiles. Luckily I remembered in time that I loved everything and everyone in the Universe, no matter how misguided, so I blew them all happy kisses, including my teacher.

 25

Somehow I managed to contain myself until lunchtime when I finally shared my huge revelation with my soulmate in the cafeteria.

"Lollie, I've just realised, I'm supposed to use my new cosmic powers to help planet Earth, and I want you come with me!"

My soulmate took a deep breath before she burst my pretty balloon. "*Carita*, I'm sorry, going back to Earth is not a good idea for you just now."

Lola still didn't know about Sky. She was just making a v. diplomatic reference to my birthday upgrade. In normal (i.e. not bonkers) circumstances, that's what I'd have heard.

But in my state of extreme cosmic loopiness, I heard something like: *The Agency would have to be clinically INSANE to send you on another mission. Letting your best FRIEND go over to the DARK Powers – they'll probably never trust you AGAIN!*

I went up the *wall*!

"You're the one who's always telling me to follow my dreams!" I blazed. "But obviously you didn't really mean it. OK, then, I'll go by MYSELF!"

I stormed off towards the secretary's office.

Lola came chasing after me. "I can see I made

you mad," she said breathlessly. "But I don't completely understand what just happened."

I was feverishly scanning the school notice board, hunting for a list of this term's field trips. They were all fully subscribed, except for one *très* obscure-sounding course: SPEND FIVE DAYS STUDYING TIME-STREAMS IN UPPER EGYPT.

I had no clue what 'time-streams' were, I just saw an opportunity to escape to Earth and share my fabulous cosmic energy with my fave planet. There were two places left. I scrabbled in my bag for a pen and signed my name bumpily at the bottom of the list.

Lola hastily read the flier over my shoulder. "Are you *nuts*! We HATED ancient Egypt."

"This course isn't in ancient Egypt," I told her loftily. "It's in my century."

I read aloud from the blurb. "'You will be based in a locally run hostel with air-con and angelic internet facilities. Your studies will only occupy a few hours a day, leaving ample free time to visit local antiquities.' I think it sounds cool!" I added defiantly.

"Boo, you do realise they're leaving at dawn tomorrow! That's practically *tonight*!"

"I know," I said happily. "Can't wait!"

That evening my soulmate cautiously popped her head round my door. "Hi!"

I looked up briefly from packing my bag. "Do you think they'll have conditioner? Maybe I should take mine in case?"

Lola took a breath. "You know you wanted me to come on your Earth mission with you? How would you feel if we both did this time-stream course?"

"Are you *kidding*? I'd LOVE it!" I gave a gasp of disappointment. "But it's too late. The office will be closed!"

Lola laughed. "Aha, but I knew that, so I just ran down to the library and used my internet skills to bag the last slot."

We jumped up and down screaming with excitement.

"But what about the concert?" I remembered. "You had that solo and everything."

"Pooh to that!" she giggled. "I'm not letting you have all those gorgeous foreign angel boys to yourself!"

Lola's pants were so on fire it's a wonder the heavenly fire brigade didn't come bursting in to hose her down there and then. Realising I was determined to leave Heaven, my unbelievably lovely and loyal friend had rushed to our teacher, who put in a high priority call to Michael. He said since they couldn't stop me going to Egypt (see previous comments on Free Will), Lola had to go with me and monitor my every move. Ignorant of this behind the scenes activity, I rushed off to help Lola pack.

"You know what?" I said emerging from her closet with an armful of cotton dresses. "I think something amazing is going to happen to me in Egypt. I got tingles in my belly button the minute I saw the word 'Egypt' on the flier."

"Yeah?" Lola was stuffing random items in her backpack.

"Totally! This is like my hot date with destiny!"

She straightened up.

"Don't take this the wrong way, but that hot date feeling isn't always what you—"

"Tell you what," I interrupted. "I'm going to run and fetch you that cute wrap dress. Blue's more your colour anyway." I flew off like an angel girl who's glugged *way* too much diet cola.

Here's what Lola would have said, if I could have come down off my whizzy pink cloud long enough to stick around and listen.

Your aura is all lit up like a Christmas tree, my loopy friend. The PODS could probably spot you from Mars. Please be VERY careful.

Here's what my inner angel would have said, if she was still open for business.

The Test is coming.

Stay home.

CHAPTER FOUR

The dawn time flight was packed with archaeology types in unattractive long shorts and floppy hats.

"And you've got your phone," Lola said for the zillionth time.

"Yes, Lola, I've got my phone," I sighed.

"And if you go *anywhere* without me, you absolutely promise to keep it switched on?"

"OK, OK, I promise!" I puffed out my cheeks.

Since I didn't know a) that I was flying without radar or b) about the Test, I couldn't imagine why Lola was being so twitchy. It's usually *me* who gets nervous before cosmic adventures.

We arrived in the simmering heat of late afternoon. Outside the time portal the noise levels practically knocked me off my feet. Bus and car horns blaring. Egyptian pop music pumping from doorways.

Technically this was the twenty-first century, but it actually felt like all the different Egyptian centuries were rubbing along merrily side by side. You could see minarets soaring like fairy tale towers above shiny hotels and modern banks. Just visible through the crumbly ruins of an old temple, was the familiar egg-yolk yellow logo of a McDonald's!

Shimmering like an angelic oasis between a noisy tourist bazaar and a small hotel was our hostel – invisible to humans, and so full of beautiful celestial vibes, no Dark agent could ever get inside.

We escaped gratefully into the air-conditioned foyer. The raucous street sounds cut out as if someone had flipped a switch.

After meeting our tutors and the other angel kids on the course, we were allocated a room on the third floor. To our relief it looked out over the tropical gardens at the back, not the dusty frantic street. French doors opened on to a small private balcony.

My friend wandered out to admire the view. "Boo, you can see the Nile from here! It looks just the same as in ancient times! Even those little boats, the *feluccas*, are the same."

We unpacked then just flopped on our beds. A slightly-too-hot breeze wafted river smells in through the open window.

I was so happy I felt like I was literally floating. I'd dreamed of going on a mission and now, quite soon, it was going to happen – I just knew it.

I beamed across at Lola. "Glad you came?"

"Oh yeah, definitely."

"I love being an angel, don't you?" I babbled. "I keep thinking it can't get any better, but it always *always* does!"

Lola nodded agreement but I saw a flicker of worry cross her face.

The sun was starting to set. One by one the amplified voices of the *muezzins* cried out from nearby minarets, calling faithful Muslims to prayer. We drifted out on to our balcony to listen.

The sun sank out of sight, leaving streaks like rosy chalk marks in the sky. I noticed a faint shimmer down by the river. Some local earth angels were sending vibes.

"We should join in," I said impulsively.

"Mel, I don't think that's such a—"

"That's why I *came*, Lollie," I insisted. "To make Earth a better place!"

33

Making Earth a better place, also lighting up the night with my sparkly new aura. Equivalent to hanging out a flashing sign saying: FORCES OF EVIL HELP YOURSELF!

Lola opened her mouth, then shut it immediately. An angel girl without her divine radar isn't exactly going to listen to your advice.

We sent vibes until the stars came out. Then we went in to get changed for the party.

There's something I want to tell you. OK, I don't exactly WANT to tell you, but there's no point telling this story unless I tell the whole truth, not just the pretty sparkly bits.

Remember that speck of darkness? Remember I said I didn't know it was there? I *knew*, OK?

I'd just put so much time and energy into hiding it, I'd very nearly fooled myself. But if you'd taken an x-ray of my soul when I arrived at the Angel Academy that's what you'd have seen, pulsing like a teeny ugly little heart, among all that swirly rainbow-coloured soul light – a living sleeping seed of pure Dark energy, waiting for the exact right moment to wake up and do maximum damage.

I'd just been sending vibes in the open air, recklessly exposing my gorgeous but highly vulnerable new energy field to Earth's deeply PODS-contaminated atmosphere. Near-perfect cosmic conditions for hatching out your own Dark angel.

No, I mean that literally. That's the Test.

It's a hot date – with your Dark side.

With absolutely no clue what was in store for me, I went on merrily trying to decide between my beaded gypsy skirt or my apple green miniskirt with appliquéd daisies. Lola was in the bathroom putting on her face.

"I'm such a fluff-brain," I called. "I'd totally forgotten Egypt is a Muslim country now! They had all those really random gods before."

This was my friend's cue to say, "Babe, you are *not* a fluff-brain. When are you going to start believing in yourself?"

What she actually said is. "*Melanie!* You can't go dissing people's *GODS!*"

For some reason Lola's reaction really upset me. I felt like she was saying I was stupid and insensitive to people's cultures.

I returned my gypsy skirt to the wardrobe with an angry jangle of coat hangers. "I wasn't dissing *anybody*," I flashed back. "I was just saying I never really got a handle on them."

My problem with the old Egyptian gods was they almost never came with their original heads, they were all like, half-cow, half-dog, half-mongoose or whatever.

Before I could explain, Lola sang out, "There weren't *so* many," and she started spouting ancient Egyptian names! "There was Bastet, the cat goddess, Hathor and Osiris, oh and Hapy the river god—"

"I *get* it," I growled, stepping into my miniskirt. "They had a LOT of gods!"

"Isis is my fave!" Lola went on, refusing to take the hint. "She was the protector of girls and women. She could be a bit violent, mind you! You wouldn't want to make her mad."

I'd come across Isis before in ancient Rome and been blown away by her genuinely sweet vibes, but I felt like if I said this now, I'd have let Lola get one up on me.

When that tiny seed of darkness wakes up, it doesn't feel tiny. It feels like a huge unfriendly force trying to fight its way out of your chest.

"If you ask me, all the Egyptian gods were equally random and equally violent!" I snarled, then

I heard the spite in my voice and stopped in bewilderment.

Lola shot out of the bathroom. "Did I say something wrong? You sounded really mad."

I had no idea what had just happened. I tweaked unhappily at my top. "I'm not mad. Have you finished in there? Because we're going to be late for the party."

Half an hour later, Lola and I were up in the hostel's roof garden, piling our plates with delicious nibbles. I was wishing I'd brought my shrug. I'd forgotten how cold nights get in the desert.

Some earth-angel musicians had arrived. One did a quick mike check in Arabic. Someone played a couple of rippling chords, then the night filled with vibey local sounds.

Over our heads, stars glittered in the African darkness like huge silver mirror balls. I caught a sweet whiff of scented jasmine and my wildly unstable system swung into Joy Mode.

"This is so cool," I gushed happily. "I'm *loving* Egypt this time."

"Me too! This food is lush!" said Lola helping herself to more dip. "And they seem sweet," she added, meaning our tutors.

"Yeah, Maryam's got a wicked sense of humour."

"She needs it with Khaled!" Lola giggled. "He's kind of dynamic, wouldn't you say?"

I waggled my eyebrows. "Kind of good looking, I'd say!"

Handsome Khaled was currently charming the socks off a group of trainees. Every few minutes his hip pocket produced an urgent blast of Egyptian pop music to let everyone know he had an incoming call. Khaled seemed to get a LOT of calls!

After we'd refilled our plates a few times, Lola said we'd better mingle.

"Do we have to?" I said nervously.

Lola reminded me that a stranger was only a friend I hadn't met yet.

"Yeah, yeah," I sighed.

I wandered around, clutching a glass of sparkling pomegranate juice. This course was a bigger deal than I'd realised. Trainees had come from all-different Heavenly schools.

I kept saying "Hi" hopefully to other trainees, but you know how it is, when you're not good in groups, you blurt it out just as they turn to greet an old friend, or else they don't hear you over the music. After what seemed like a *très* long half hour, Lola came to find me, looking flushed and happy. "Isn't this great?"

"Fantastic," I fibbed enthusiastically.

"I've been talking to one of the musicians. He says we lucked out getting on to this course. Khaled and Maryam are *the* time-stream teachers apparently."

"Wow," I said.

"There's still some kids to come from the celestial college. They had a portal malfunction but they should be here by tomorrow." Lola gave me a nudge. "Celestial *college*? Indigo's school?"

I pulled a face. "I doubt he'll show. The heat would muss up his hair!"

Lola giggled. "That's so mean!"

Indigo was a v. posey boy Reuben and I met on our soul retrieval course. Reubs was convinced he fancied me.

My friend couldn't stop herself bopping to the beat. "Don't you LOVE this band? If Reubs was here, he'd be up there jamming. Wouldn't mind jamming with them myself..."

"Go for it," I told her.

Lola looked torn. "You wouldn't mind? It'd just be one song."

"Go!" I gave her a friendly push

I watched her threading her way through the party goers. We'd been in Egypt five hours max, yet Lola felt confident enough to jump up on stage and strut her stuff with a bunch of foreign musicians. Everyone would love her. They always did.

Here I was at the exact same party, totally alone. Suddenly I couldn't bear to stay and watch.

My flip-flops made pathetic slapping sounds as I hurried from the roof garden. Lola would look for me in the middle of her song and wonder where I'd gone.

As I reached the bottom of the steps, a flicker of white lightning silently lit up the sky, followed by another. Must be a storm somewhere in the desert. I was shivering in my thin top but I stayed where I was, watching the dramatic cosmic light show. It felt like the storm and I were rushing to meet each other, like we'd been travelling towards each other forever.

Are you willing to go for gold? Are you truly an angel – or was that just a beautiful dream?

In just a few hours now I was going to find out.

CHAPTER FIVE

"You were yelling, babe, are you OK?"

I woke briefly to find Lola peering anxiously into my face, then got sucked down into a new dream where Sky was getting v. excited about her new job.

"I'm working on a really special perfume counter," she kept telling me. "Can you believe I get to make the perfumes myself!"

Next thing I heard someone calling my name.

I sat up with a gasp, but the voice must have been in my dream. Lola was still sound asleep, one bare brown foot sticking out from under the sheet.

With that strangely familiar voice still ringing in my ears, I softly opened the door on to the balcony and went out. It was so early, the palm trees looked like pencil sketches waiting to be coloured in.

Someone came sauntering into my line of vision, talking on her phone. "Yeah, finally! No, not yet. OK, baby cakes, I'll let you know how it goes. Call you later, byee!"

I was practically hanging off the balcony. Not only did this angel girl have my style of talking, she even had my daffy giggle. It sounds vain, but I was mad-keen to know if she looked like me too. Don't they say everyone has a cosmic double?

The fuzzy pre-dawn light made it hard to see her properly, as she wandered off through the garden in the direction of the river.

I remember how her trainers left dark furrows in the dew.

At no point had she looked up, yet all the time I was watching I had the strangest feeling, like she totally knew I was there.

Thirty minutes later, I was trailing my arm over the side of a stylish white jeep enjoying the cool rush of air.

Lola and I were squashed in the back seat with two angel girls called Yoko and Tegan. Yoko's boyfriend was up front with Maryam. The other trainees were following in the tour bus with the delayed celestial college kids.

Lola hadn't said anything about me leaving the party. I'd asked her if she had a good time. She said fabulous, thanks. End of conversation.

We passed a cluster of flat-roofed houses surrounded by a patchwork of tiny fields. Men and women were at work in the early morning cool, throwing bundles of straw into a cart. Except for a satellite dish on the side of one of the houses, it could have been any time in the last thousand years.

Yoko and Tegan said they'd been having weird dreams all night long. Maryam said it was probably the local vibes. Apparently Egypt was well-known for giving you a hyperactive dream life.

Our tutor half-turned to us, smiling. "Ancient Egyptian temples often had a Corridor of Dreams. Humans would rent a room there for the night, hoping the gods would send a dream to shed light on their problems."

I shivered. The conversation had broken my first dream; not the one about Sky and the perfume, the one that made me yell in my sleep.

I was back in my old school hall taking an exam, but every time I tried to read the question paper to find out what *type* of exam exactly, a freak wind came whooshing out of nowhere and blew it away!

Suddenly all the lights went out, and these terrifying beings, half-divine, half-animal, were storming towards me, kicking over the desks.

"In ancient times, angels and gods did occasionally work together," Maryam was saying to the others. "Not often, just when something of real cosmic importance was at stake."

"Not now though?" I said shuddering, picturing those exam hall monsters with their scary beast heads. "We don't join forces now?"

We heard cheerful toots as the tour bus scorched past in a yellow cloud of dust. Khaled was in the driver's seat, pulling mad faces.

Maryam sighed. "He is so competitive."

Then her foot hit the accelerator so hard the jeep's wheels spun in the sand. Relieved to be distracted from bad dreams and surreal old-style gods, I joined in blowing cheeky kisses to Khaled as we surged past the bus and into the lead under a cloudless African sky.

Eventually our jeep lurched to a standstill by a grove of dusty date palms. Maryam switched off the engine. In the sudden hush, the only sounds were the clicking of palm fronds and the slap-slap of the Nile against its banks. Maryam was serenely smoothing down her headscarf as the bus pulled up alongside.

Trainees began piling off. The celestial college kids were easy to spot in their vintage-style tropical threads.

Lola nudged me. "Can you see Indigo?"

"I told you already," I sighed. "This isn't his kind of thing!"

Khaled sprinted over, jamming his phone in his pocket as he ran. "I decided to let Maryam win," he beamed.

"He let me win last time too," Maryam told us in a stage whisper. "And the time before that and—"

Khaled interrupted her breezily. "All that matters is we have reached today's time-stream site! Ladies and gentlemen, welcome to the ancient town of Seshet!"

We clambered out doubtfully, clutching our bottles of water.

I'd been hoping for an atmospheric ruin, but there wasn't even a pile of stones to show humans had lived in this desolate place.

"You are feeling cheated, I can tell!" Khaled beamed, obviously enjoying our disappointment. "Why has he dragged us out into the desert to look at nothing! But once you've mastered time-streaming, you will be seeing with different eyes!" He gestured at the desert. "What would you say if I told you that under this sand, the streets of long ago Seshet silently wait to be discovered, as they have waited for centuries?"

The idea of a buried city instantly perked everyone up.

We spent the next half hour or so wandering around the site, as our tutors pointed out where major buildings would have been, like the temple and the house of mummification and whatever.

"Over there on the outer limits was the Street of Leather Workers." Khaled waved vaguely. "A very smelly street I'm afraid! Where you are standing, Melanie and Lola, was a street with much pleasanter smells, the Street of Perfume Blenders!"

"They had a *street* of perfumers?" Lola said enviously.

Khaled beamed at her. "Didn't you know? For thousands of years Egypt was like the perfume counter of the ancient world?"

Perfume counter. A tiny shiver went down my backbone. Our tutor had used almost the exact words Sky had used in my dream.

"And as Khaled was just about to say, the best blenders were usually women!" Maryam pointed out mischievously.

Khaled pretended to mop his forehead. "Yes, sorry, almost got myself in big trouble there! And by the way, these female blenders guarded their secrets very fiercely. You might be interested to know that a Seshet perfumer was once commissioned to create a perfume for Queen Nefertiti." He noticed a few blank faces. "Have you all heard of Nefertiti?"

"I know she was pretty," Yoko said shyly.

Khaled made a tisking sound. "No, Nefertiti was not pretty. She was the most beautiful woman the world has ever seen! She ruled Egypt with her husband, the Pharaoh Akhenaten, more than three thousand years ago. They were an extremely eccentric couple, possibly a little bit mad!"

I imagined the perfume maker sleepily opening up her shop one morning, to find a royal messenger waiting on her step with a summons to design an exclusive fragrance for the supernaturally beautiful, possibly a little bit mad, Queen Nefertiti.

"Does anyone know what was *in* Nefertiti's perfume?" an angel girl asked in a hopeful voice.

Maryam laughed. "Women have been asking that for centuries! The blender had to swear to keep the ingredients secret on pain of death. This perfume was for Nefertiti and only her until the end of time."

"Was it really special?" Lola asked wistfully.

"It would seem so!" smiled Maryam. "Apparently no man could refuse her anything when she wore it."

I pictured the lovely Nefertiti removing a golden stopper from an exquisite glass bottle, dabbing a single precious drop behind her ear, and calmly going about her day leaving a trail of dazzled males.

Khaled sneaked a hasty glance at his watch, "However, we didn't bring you to Seshet to speak of perfume. Being virtually untouched by the twenty-first century, this site is an ideal place to practice time-stream skills for the first time."

Several kids whipped out their palm pilots, but Khaled said we didn't need to take notes. "Time-stream theory can be summed up in a simple sentence," he smiled. "*Vibes never die.*"

Khaled explained that every soul has its special cosmic signature, a totally unique vibe. Because vibes don't die, you can still detect that special vibe in the planet's energy field centuries after the soul in question has left his or her human body. Not just that, once you learn to tune into someone's soul vibes, you can literally see events from their life playing over again, like a cosmic DVD!

"But really, why go to so much trouble?" Khaled asked us. "In times gone by, sure, but we have made technological advances since then. We can program a capsule to take us to a specific moment in history and see these events unfolding in real time. Why do it the hard way?"

"To make us more effective celestial agents?" suggested someone.

Everyone hooted. Every time our teachers make us do something that strikes us as completely pointless, they *always* say it will make us more effective agents!

Maryam looked amused. "Khaled and I could give you a long list of reasons why acquiring time-stream skills is a good thing, but hopefully you'll discover them for yourselves!"

As this was our first attempt, we were allowed to work with someone we knew. I grabbed Lola and we found ourselves a patch of shade under a date palm.

"Once upon a time, trainees learned time-stream skills as a matter of course," Maryam told us. "After they had mastered the more advanced techniques, they would be taught how to use them to travel through time."

"Don't worry," Khaled put in with his warm smile, "we won't be asking you to attempt time travel today!"

We had to get into a comfortable sitting position and link hands with our partner. We were instructed to keep our eyes open, as Maryam got us to imagine we were floating in a vast ocean of cosmic energy, with multicoloured currents swirling this way and that. These were the time-streams. Since Nefertiti's name had come up, our brief was to try to pick up this ancient queen's time-stream.

Lola and I cleared our minds, focusing on Maryam's quiet instructions.

Her voice started getting oddly faint and fuzzy, like she was talking inside a badly tuned radio. Soon I could hardly hear her, though I could hear my own breathing perfectly clearly. My body felt relaxed and strangely heavy like I was falling asleep. But I wasn't asleep. My mind was clearly excited to be using this unfamiliar new muscle. I could feel it swooping happily from one time-stream to another, like a swallow chasing gnats, getting closer and closer to our target.

Yes!

As if someone had flipped a dimmer switch, the morning sunshine faded to twilight. Same river, totally different millennium. You could just tell. For a long while nothing happened, then I heard a splash or I saw a movement. Something.

A ghostly shape shot into view, some kind of boat travelling super-fast.

Powered by the oars of sweating slaves, (we couldn't see them, but we could feel their vibes) the boat glided almost silently into the shore. Someone lit a lantern and we caught thrilling glints of gold. Talk about beginner's luck! We'd only got Queen Nefertiti's royal barge!

A slave splashed softly across to the bank to make the boat safe, then carefully manoeuvred a plank into position. Shadowy figures came down the plank. We heard low voices.

"I hope you remembered the gold for the watchman, Adjo? And everyone knows what they're doing?"

"*Yes*, Baraka, we know what we're doing!"

"Mardian says as we go back up the Nile, news will spread. People will soon be volunteering their support."

"He'd better hope the news doesn't spread to the Roman barracks!" commented someone.

"We're not risking our lives for Mardian," the first voice reminded them. "We're doing it for Egypt and for Cleopatra!"

Our vision vanished in a storm of pixels.

"Bums!" Lola moaned. "We got the wrong queen!"

And not just any wrong queen. I was shaken to the core at this cosmic coincidence. With four thousand plus years of Egyptian royalty to choose from, we somehow had to zoom in on Sky's fave royal, Queen Cleopatra.

Maryam hurried over. "Is everything OK?"

Lola and I explained in whispers. "We did it like you said, truly," I told her. "How come we got it wrong?"

"I don't know that you got it wrong. It was a little unexpected that's all," Maryam said gently.

Not only did we *not* get Nefertiti, but when we shared our experiences later with the group, we discovered we were a humiliating 1300 years off target!

It probably wasn't a real time-stream at all, I thought gloomily. We had the Nile in front of us so we just automatically imagined a glamorous royal barge.

But why would Lola and I specifically imagine *Cleopatra's* barge? And why would we *both* come up with a scenario of loyal courtiers sneaking into Seshet on some hush-hush mission? And how come we cooked up someone called Mardian, a name neither of us had heard before in our lives?

Back at the hostel a buffet lunch had been set up in a cool airy courtyard. Lola and I were trying to decide where to sit when Maryam and Khaled beckoned us over. It turned out they thought we'd picked up on a genuinely Cleopatra-related time-stream. The clincher was that name 'Mardian'.

"Cleopatra's most trusted adviser was a eunuch called Mardian." Maryam explained.

Of course I had to be the one to ask what a eunuch was!

Sorry if this grosses you out, but apparently, some ancient Egyptian parents deliberately had their boy children 'altered' as my nan used to say, a v. drastic operation which humans only carry out on farm animals or tom cats in my time.

Not being ancient Egyptian myself, I found this hard to grasp, but parents actually did this to help their sons get on in the world. Then they could be taken on by important families as tutors, private secretaries or whatever, without the worry of big sex scandals.

"Since a eunuch couldn't marry or have children, his work became his whole life," Maryam told us. "Highly educated eunuchs, like Mardian, often secured good positions at court. Mardian had known Cleopatra since they were children. He was devoted to her and worked tirelessly for his country."

"Wasn't she a bit of a minx?" I asked, remembering Sky's story.

Khaled laughed. "You've heard how she made Julius Caesar fall in love with her?"

I nodded. "She had herself smuggled into her own palace in a rug."

"She knew how to use her charms to her advantage, that one!" Maryam chuckled. "After they'd become lovers, Cleopatra made Caesar promise he would never invade Egypt. They had a little boy together, Caesarian, which means Little Caesar. Unfortunately Caesar was assassinated in Rome a few years later. Once again Cleopatra and her kingdom were vulnerable to Rome. The new leaders distrusted this feisty Egyptian queen and summoned her to go to Tarsus, to appear before Mark Antony and answer for her 'crimes' against Rome."

"Her advisors begged her not to go, saying she'd be sailing to her certain death," explained Khaled. "But Cleopatra had a special reason for wanting to go. She and Mark Antony had what you'd call a *history*."

Maryam took over the story. "They had met just once when he was a young captain and she was only twelve or thirteen. He was at a state banquet her father, the eccentric King Auletes, was giving for the Romans.

During the meal, the king got very drunk. He got up in the middle of a speech by one of the Roman VIPs, and danced all by himself. Mark Antony guessed how humiliated the young princess was feeling, and took the trouble to talk to her, asking her opinions, putting her at her ease, treating her not like a little girl but like the great queen she would one day become. She never forgot his kindness."

"Her feelings for Mark Antony weren't the only reason Cleopatra decided to go to Tarsus," Khaled added hastily. "She was a woman, but first and foremost she was a queen, and she had thought of an extraordinary way to turn this meeting to her own advantage, saving herself, her throne and her country." Khaled smiled at me and Lola. "This is where your vision comes in! Cleopatra's plan could only succeed if she had her people's help. She secretly sent messengers to every town in Egypt to seek out the best goldsmiths and glassworkers, the best entertainers..."

"They had to keep Cleopatra's plan under wraps," Maryam put in. "Rome had legions stationed in Egypt as part of their build-up to a military invasion. There were spies everywhere."

"Omigosh," I breathed. "Those guys were *auditioning* to see who got the royal contract!"

"Did her plan work?" asked Lola.

Maryam nodded, smiling. "Cleopatra saved Egypt *and* made Mark Anthony fall in love with her."

Ooh-la la, I thought. That girl bowled men over like skittles!

"So what *was* this amazing plan?" Lola's eyes glinted. This whole Cleopatra story had her hooked. But Maryam and Khaled had to go off to a meeting.

"Maybe you'll be able to locate the same time-stream before we finish the course," Maryam suggested, smiling. "Then you'll find out for yourself!"

CHAPTER SIX

Our time-stream sessions were scheduled for early morning or evening, when cosmic vibes are at their most pure.

This left me and Lola with our afternoons free to do the tourist thing. As it turned out, my soulmate had arranged a v. special surprise.

When we came down into the foyer, the earth-angel boy on the desk shot out into the broiling street and gave a piercing whistle.

A horse-drawn *caleche* rattled up to the door. The driver in his traditional flowing *djellaba* had to be the toughest looking earth angel I'd ever seen: short, bald and absolutely unsmiling!

"Mel, meet Mohammed!" Lola beamed, adding in a whisper, "I thought it would be fun to play princesses for an afternoon!"

I did feel exactly like a princess as Mohammed silently handed us up into our hired carriage. A hot sweaty princess but who cares?

We snapped crazy pictures of each other under our fringed canopy, as Mohammed took us clip clopping through the town at higher speeds than you might naturally expect a horse and buggy to go!

Egyptian traffic is MAD: pedestrians, donkey-carts, bikes, trucks and buses all competing for the same space. At junctions Mohammed stood up like an old-style chariot driver, glowering over the mayhem, before hurtling off in his chosen direction.

Now and then he'd stop without warning, obviously expecting us to get out and wander around some suitable tourist attraction.

Like nice polite angel girls we did what we were told. We checked out a couple of local bazaars, and peeked shyly into a cafe where old men were smoking hubble-bubble pipes and having heated discussions, reading aloud to each other from Egyptian newspapers to back up their arguments.

Last on Mohammed's private checklist was the local museum.

Can I be totally honest? I'm not a museums kind of girl. I get inside and I'm like – what am I supposed to be looking at again?

But as Mohammed was making it perfectly clear he was settling down for a long snooze, in we went.

We walked through dimly lit rooms past showcases filled with King Whosit's second best chariot and whatever, and after five minutes, like usual, I was slowly losing the will to live. But after ten minutes, I was like, Uh-oh. Houston we have a problem.

Having acquired the knack of picking up time-streams I couldn't seem to stop! The tiniest object would set an ancient Egyptian movie running in my head – and museums have a LOT of objects as you know. Also, just to increase the stress levels a notch, human tourists were constantly walking through us, a v. common angelic experience, but one I personally could do without.

I trailed after my friend, getting increasingly spaced, but not wanting to seem feeble, you know how it is. I was literally on the verge of passing out when I saw a sign. TO THE MUMMY ROOM.

Now I'm very nearly as fascinated by old mummies as I am by museums, but at that moment the scientifically-temperature-controlled mummy chamber seemed *hugely* desirable, mainly because it was blissfully free of humans.

"I'm going to check out the mummy," I mumbled.

Lola's eyes went wide. "Melanie! I can feel its vibes from *here*."

With my divine radar on the fritz, I wasn't thinking vibes, I was just thinking cool, empty.

"You're on your own, Boo!" Lola called. Her voice had a panicky edge. "I've got a phobia of mummies, remember?"

"Won't be long," I quavered.

Black spots danced before my eyes as I tottered up the steps. By then, of course, it was too late.

I could see myself reflected in the glass, an averagely pretty angel girl wearing a white cotton dress over cropped white cotton leggings – and an expression of growing horror.

Inside the glass case, propped up like a scarecrow in what must once have been a sumptuous, silk-lined coffin, was the dried-up shell of – I suppose the polite expression would be – a 'former human being'.

I don't know why the mummy was more disturbing than an average corpse but trust me, it was. All its bandages had rotted down to shreds, allowing its jaws to fall open, reminding me of a dead dog I'd seen once in Park Hall High Street. The mummy's accidental leer exposed the stumps of four-thousand-year-old teeth.

Then some vague survival instinct kicked in and I flew out of that chamber like a baby bunny with its tail on fire.

Unfortunately I shot through the wrong door, finding myself in a bewildering corridor with offshoots going every which way.

Like my friend I was now seriously mummy phobic, so I couldn't even *think* of going back. I just kept running, getting more and more lost, until I ran into a completely empty part of the museum. Empty of humans anyway.

Thoughtfully studying a display of ancient jewellery was the angel girl I'd seen from my balcony.

Do you ever have those dreams where you know exactly what's going to happen next? She'll turn and smile, I thought, and it'll be like we've known each other forever.

The mysterious angel girl turned, flashing a wonderfully familiar smile. "*I'm* sorry," she said as if we were in mid-conversation. "Why would *anyone* want to wear some gruesome old bluebottle on a chain?"

The similarity in our voices should have spooked me but it was actually the opposite. I felt fabulously safe, like I already knew everything about her. I pointed to a notice inside the showcase.

"It's called THE FLIES OF VALOUR. It was a medal given for great courage in battle."

She gave a scream of laughter. "They had a *medal* called the Flies of Valour?! How completely hilarious! Do you think they had one called the Cockroach of Loyalty or the Maggot of – I don't know—?"

"Majesty?" I suggested with a smirk.

"'The Maggot of Majesty'! Ooh I like it!"

She wasn't my physical double. She was too pretty to be my double. But in every other way she was my twin; her gestures, her sassy way of talking, even her little wrap dress and leggings were identical, except her outfit was brilliant poppy red.

She wagged her finger accusingly. "You don't remember me!"

"I do, I saw you early this morning," I confessed shyly.

"I know! You'd be such a rubbish spy," she giggled. "No, before that, Babe! We were on the

63

same Soul-Retrieval course. Not that you'd notice me with gorgeous Indigo schmoozing around!"

I felt myself going pink. "I don't think I saw you at our first time-stream session—" I said hastily changing the subject.

She shrugged. "I didn't get here till, like, five this morning, so I grabbed a few minutes shuteye."

"Wow, so you and Indigo must be at the same school? What's it like at the celestial coll—?"

But she was already dancing on to the next showcase.

"*Finally* some jewellery a girl can relate to!" she bubbled. "I LOVE this gold ankh, don't you?"

An ankh, if you didn't know, is shaped like a cross except it has a loop thingy at the top. On our Egyptian field trip, Mr Allbright had explained that the loop let everybody know that this powerful sacred symbol belonged strictly to the gods, and was only, like, on *loan* to humans.

This particular ankh was made of solid gold studded with glittering dark gems. I thought it looked v. scary, but I dutifully said, "Wow."

"Do you want it?" The angel girl impulsively stretched out her hand. I thought she was going to put it right through the glass!

She let out her contagious giggle. "Too slow, you lost out!"

I laughed nervously, not sure if she was making fun.

"I've had enough of this graveyard," she said abruptly. "How about you, Mel Beeby?"

"Definitely!" I giggled, secretly flattered that she'd remembered my name from the course.

We emerged from the air-conditioned museum into a solid wall of heat. We both started fanning ourselves at the same moment, which made us laugh.

"Sorry, I don't know your name," I said.

The girl's eyes sparkled, as if she'd been hoping I'd ask. "It's Maia!" She pronounced it to rhyme with liar.

"Maia is my favourite name," I told her shyly but she was checking her watch and didn't hear.

"Fancy hooking up later?" she asked casually.

"Totally," I beamed. "I know Lola would love to meet you."

Her smooth forehead puckered in a frown. "Yeah, but it's you I'm asking, OK?"

"OK," I said, startled.

Maia was watching me with an oddly detached expression. "How come you have such a low opinion of yourself, babe?"

I felt myself going hot and cold. "I didn't think I did."

She shook her head. "No, I totally read people, and I bet – did you say your friend's name is Lola? I bet *Lola* gets to play superstar twenty-four-seven, am I right?" Maia shook her head pityingly. "No fun always being the understudy is it, sweetie?"

"Actually, Lola's my best friend, so please don't talk about her like that," I said angrily. The words just came out by themselves. I'm usually rubbish at standing up to people, but she'd crossed a line.

Maia went white. "That so didn't come out how I meant. I'm so sorry. I'm so, so sorry." She totally didn't know where to look.

I was already intrigued by this unusual angel girl. Now a tiny door in my heart that I hadn't known was there, flew wide open.

Maia might act sassy, but she had just shown me that she was every bit as scared and vulnerable as – well, *me*.

I touched her arm. "It's OK, really."

"Are you sure?" Enormous tears hung off the ends of her eyelashes, threatening to fall.

"Totally sure, and I'd still love to meet up."

She was fiddling with something at her throat. With a twang of shock I recognised the ankh.

Maia saw my face. "What? This?" She lifted the jewel-studded pendant, peering down almost in surprise. "No way! You thought I nicked it from the museum! That's so hilarious!"

My face was burning. "I didn't really—"

"Sweetie, this is fake. I bought it in Ambrosia before I came!"

"I honestly didn't—" I was beside myself with shame to think I'd virtually accused another angel of stealing.

"Hey, it was a natural mistake, don't stress it!" Maia had taken out her phone. She started walking away.

"Come back with us!" I offered wildly. "You and Lola would totally hit it off, I know you would!"

"Stuff to do, babe!" she called. "Later, OK!"

"But how will I find you?" I shouted.

"I'll find you, OK!"

Lola picked that moment to come flying out of the museum. She arrived on the pavement, looking frazzled.

"Hi babe!" I greeted her. "Did you see that cool angel girl I was with?"

She practically snapped my head off.

"No I didn't! Where the sassafras did you get to? I've been worried sick!"

I scanned the crowded pavements, wanting to point out my fascinating new friend, but Maia must have been a fast walker because there was no sign of a sassy angel girl in a poppy red dress.

CHAPTER SEVEN

Back at the hostel Lola went right off the deep end.

"You just *disappeared*, Melanie! I had NO idea what had happened! AND you forgot to keep your phone switched on!"

"Jeez, Lollie, you sound like my mum!"

"I don't CARE! Suppose the PODS had got you."

"You really think the Powers of Darkness would let me make a *phone* call!"

"That's NOT the point!" Lola was so upset she'd given herself hiccups.

"Don't let's fight," I pleaded. "I don't want us to fight."

I fetched us both a cool drink from our mini fridge, and we took them out on to the balcony. I made Lola hold her breath and block her ears and eventually her hiccups stopped and we were friends again.

"You're still coming tonight, aren't you?" she asked anxiously.

My soulmate had arranged to do a couple of sets with the band.

I nodded enthusiastically. "Yeah! Wouldn't miss it, truly."

A voice in my head whispered: *Maia might be there.*

Lola was just getting into her second number, when I heard a friendly BEEP from inside my bag. I felt a happy little buzz when I saw Maia's text message.

Wait 4 u downstairs. Maz.

Far too excited to wonder how she got my number, I rushed off.

At the bottom of the steps, I heard a stifled giggle and Maia sprang out. "Surrender innocent angel girl, I am your worst nightmare!"

We both burst out laughing. We'd picked almost identical outfits again: floaty gypsy skirts with beaded tops. I was in apple blossom pinks and greens, and Maia was in glittery sophisticated black.

"You should really go to the party looking like that," I said admiringly.

"No way! Can't take those types of get togethers. They're so totally bogus."

I felt a naughty thrill go up my spine. Maia was saying we were the real deal, the rebels. Everyone else was just 'bogus'.

She was scrutinising me again. "You trust me, don't you?"

"Totally," I said, ignoring a far-off twang of alarm.

"Only I'm going to take you to this really special place, but it's a surprise so you'll have to cover your eyes."

Giggling nervously, I let Maia steer me through the gardens. Belly-dancing music drifted from a tourist boat. I could hear loud rhythmic clapping as the tourists joined in the dance.

I heard Maia snigger. "Just picture all those old wrinklies doing belly-dancing moves! Euw!"

"Don't be mean," I protested, giggling. "And don't make me laugh, I keep nearly tripping over as it is!"

The Nile smells were getting much stronger. We must have been getting close to the river. I could hear Maia breathing and I felt a rush of panic. Was she planning to push me in?

"Duck!" she commanded, letting me go.

I ducked through an invisible entrance, setting off tinkling sounds.

"You can look now!"

"How – where—?" I stuttered amazed. "What *is* this place?"

"It belongs to the hostel. No one uses it so I thought we'd take it over." Maia seemed pleased at my surprise.

Tea-lights in pretty glass holders flickered everywhere. Three walls were hung with richly patterned Bedouin rugs, the fourth wall was mostly taken up by a huge open window overlooking the Nile. Under the window a squashy sofa, draped with more tribal rugs, just begged you to kick off your flip-flops and enjoy the river views.

"Someone must come here, or who lit the little tea-lights?"

"That was me, silly! I wanted it to be special." Maia put on a girly voice. "Hi, madam, my name is Maia and I'll be looking after your every need this evening."

I giggled. "You're TOTALLY mad, you know that!"

She got busy throwing fresh mint into a pot, making Egyptian-style mint tea, seeming to know exactly where everything was kept.

We curled up with our steaming tea glasses, watching the stars dance in the water.

Maia noticed me shiver. "Wrap yourself in one of these!" She helped me arrange one of the tribal rugs around my shoulders. "Isn't this better than that old party?" She gave a naughty giggle. "You'd like it even better if you were with Indigo!"

"I wasn't *that* into him, shut up!"

Maia went so quiet I thought I'd offended her. She fiddled with her fake ankh.

"Actually, Indigo isn't the only mate we have in common." Maia sounded cagy. "Your friend Lola is going out with an old friend of mine."

I laughed, amazed. "No way! You really know Brice!"

Maia suddenly got off the sofa and went to sit in a nearby wicker chair, I heard her take a breath. "I probably seem really sure of myself, right? Sassy, quirky...?"

"Well, yeah—"

"It's totally put on. I'm just so sick of getting hurt."

I sat up, startled. "Omigosh, Maia."

She sounded almost angry. "It's always the same story. I make friends with some cool angel girl. We swap

73

girly info, fave music, most embarrassing moments. Finally I take a risk and tell her something real, you know, like the truth about my past, and suddenly little Miss Celestial Cool doesn't want to know."

"Maia, that's terrib—"

"Let me say it, before I chicken out. I wasn't telling the whole truth just now. Brice and I do go way back, but we didn't exactly meet in Heaven."

"Oh, wow, you're from the same time period?" I breathed.

She shook her head. "We didn't meet on Earth either."

With the sick, dropping down a lift-shaft feeling that goes with real shock, I realised what she was telling me. Maia had met Brice in the exact OPPOSITE of Heaven; in the clammy sulphur-smelling corridors of a Hell school.

I heard her swallow. "I don't blame you if you don't want to be my friend. You'd always be thinking, 'Is Maia for real?'" She sounded like a lost little girl.

I was shocked, I won't deny it.

Then I thought, Get real, Mel! Did you honestly think Brice was the only cosmic dropout in the Universe?

If I've learned one thing from knowing Brice, it's not to judge anybody ever again.

"I would be proud to be your friend, Maia," I told her. "I think you're *really* brave to be so upfront. Everyone deserves a second chance, no matter what they did."

Maia's eyes filled with a sudden strange longing. "You don't mean that?"

"I do mean it, Maia! If I get the chance I'm going to tell those pinheaded angel girls at your school what I think of them! They should be supporting you, not treating you like a cosmic outcast!"

Maia let out a half-sob. "You're amazing, you know that? No wonder Indigo thinks you're lovely."

I felt my heart skip a beat. "Indigo thinks I'm *lovely*?"

She giggled tearily. "Are you kidding? Know what he told his best mate?"

We were getting to know each other so fast, I felt almost drunk. As we talked on into the night, I started to feel strangely blurry at the edges, as if I couldn't tell where I ended and Maia began. She'd taken such a risk, sharing her dark secret, it seemed like I owed her one in return.

So I told her about my biggest ever failure as an angel. I told her about me and Sky.

When I got back to our room, Lola was sitting up in bed reading.

"Didn't you get my texts?" she demanded. "You should have got one. I sent about a *zillion*."

My excitement fizzled out like a dud firework.

I was such a bad friend. Not only had I abandoned Lola in a strange country two nights in a row, I'd shared personal info with Maia that I was still keeping back from my best friend.

I didn't say any of this. That would have been the sensible thing to do. I just tried to laugh it off. "I didn't get any texts," I said brightly. "We must have been in a cosmic black spot."

"What were you *doing* though, wandering around all by yourself at this time of night?"

"I wasn't alone," I protested. "I ran into Maia, that angel girl I told you about. She took me to the coolest place. You'd love it!"

Lola shut her book with a snap. "Is that right?"

"She goes to Indigo's school. Apparently she knows Brice really well."

I didn't explain *how* Maia came to know Brice. That was Maia's secret, plus she'd made me promise faithfully not to tell.

"Seems weird I haven't seen her about." Lola was punching her pillow with more force than strictly necessary.

"Why's it weird? Maia doesn't like crowds that's all. Not everyone is a big show-off like you, you know!"

The cruel words just burst out.

Lola quickly switched off her lamp. Her voice sounded incredibly hurt. "You should get some sleep. We've got another early start."

No fun always being the understudy, is it, sweetie? whispered Maia's voice in my head.

"It's not really up to you when I go to sleep, is it?" I snapped. Pointedly switching on my lamp, I picked up my shiny new paperback and settled down to read.

CHAPTER EIGHT

My book was still lying open on my face when Lola's alarm clock jangled us awake two hours later.

I managed to get myself washed, dressed and on to the tour bus, by telling myself my new friend would be there.

She didn't show. As the bus doors slid shut, I felt really confused. I'd assumed she'd be as keen to see me as I was to see her. I didn't know what to think. Was it something I said?

I thought of calling Maia back on her mobile but Lola was beside me, stony faced. She hadn't said a word since we got up. It wasn't such a long drive to the time site, but with my friend giving me the big silent treatment, it seemed a LOT longer.

It was technically morning by the time we arrived at the temple, but the sun stayed stubbornly behind yellowish cloud.

We climbed up crumbling steps between rows of weather-beaten statues depicting Egyptian gods wearing that bizarre headgear that always reminds me of space helmets.

The temple was mostly rubble. Just four giant sand-coloured pillars were left, towering over us like massive trees, making me feel like a pointless little ant.

Khaled made us examine the base of one of the pillars, where someone had carved exquisite lotus flowers from the stone. If you squinted you could make out speckles of sky blue on one of the lotus petals, the one ancient Egyptian colour to survive centuries of desert storms.

Even though I felt so down, I felt a tiny buzz of excitement to think I'd be seeing this dust-coloured ruin restored to its original blues, greens and glittering gold, assuming I managed to find a time-stream.

I had to work with Yoko this time, but I had soo much trouble focusing you wouldn't believe. A spiteful desert breeze had sprung up, stirring up flurries of sand that stung your eyes and any exposed bits of skin. But I think my problems were mostly down to my mixed-up state of mind.

Because Maia hadn't showed up, and I had no idea why, I was feeling more and more uneasy about our evening together. Specifically, I felt I shouldn't have talked about Sky. I felt like I'd betrayed her to Maia, which was dumb, because how was Sky ever going to find out?

But I commanded my mind to become as quiet and empty as a cloudless sky, like Mr Allbright always tells us, and after a few minutes, Yoko and I started getting quite cute cosmic footage of temple dancing girls. (By the way, the colours of the temple were AMAZING!)

Suddenly the deep hush of the temple was disturbed by creepy scrabblings.

I started picturing that gruesome mummy, clawing its way out of a forgotten tomb. It did NOT improve my concentration let me tell you!

Everyone was struggling to stay tuned to their time-streams. Everyone except Lola.

"Sorry," she said to her partner. She walked over to a stone alcove, removed bits of rubble from an ancient storm drain and gently lifted out a tiny spotted kitten by its scruff.

"Sorry," Lola said, to our teachers this time. "It was stuck."

Khaled came over to admire the wild kitten. "She might actually be descended from the original temple cats!" he smiled. "See these spotted markings, and the slight tuftiness to the ears? You can see almost identical animals in ancient tomb paintings."

He went on about the intense spiritual connection Egyptians had with cats, and their belief that cats were like, the 'eyes of the gods', maybe because cats' eyes glow so spookily in the dark.

But it was really Lola who had everyone's attention. The other trainees were giving her wondering smiles, thinking how special she was.

No fun always being the understudy, sweetie.

"How did you know it was there?" I asked Lola jealously when we were back on the bus.

"I just did," she said tersely and went back to staring out the window. Then I heard her take a breath and it all came tumbling out.

"You think I'm jealous of Maia," she hissed, "but I'm SO not! I just think it's a bit weird that she signed up for this course, then doesn't come on any of the trips. And she says she knows Brice, but he's definitely never mentioned her to me."

"What's really a bit weird, Lola," I flashed back, "is that you're so quick to get your knives into someone you haven't even MET."

Again, it wasn't what I said, it was the poisonous way I said it.

Lola went white. She actually had tears in her eyes, but it's like she had to finish what she'd started. "Just answer me one question, Mel," she pleaded, "then I swear I'll let it drop." She took a breath. "Has anyone but you actually *seen* this angel girl?"

I was furious. "You're unbelievable, Lola, you know that? You go swanning off with strange musicians and that's fine. But if someone actually wants to be my friend, it's like a major cosmic catastrophe!"

We travelled the rest of the way in grim silence. A scary space had opened up between us, and anything we said would have just made it worse.

Back at the hostel the staff were hastily bringing in tables and chairs from the courtyard. It was too windy now to eat outside.

The dining room was hideously stuffy even with the ceiling fans whirring. Occasionally a plastic chair would go bowling past the window, jolting me out of my thoughts.

Maybe Maia just couldn't face those snotty celestial college girls? Or maybe it was me she couldn't face? I'd said I wanted to be her friend, but probably she'd heard it all before.

I waited till Lola went up to help herself to seconds, then sneakily tried Maia's number. All I got was a strange robot voice saying her phone was switched off.

Lola and I spent our free afternoon sullenly reading on our beds, with the net curtains whipping in the wind. Forgetting we were scheduled for a return trip to Seshet at sunset, we both fell asleep.

By the time we struggled upright, the winds had grown so strong our hostel was thrumming like some strange musical instrument.

We splashed water on our faces, grabbed two bottles of water from the mini fridge, rushed back for our phones, then zoomed downstairs, all in deadly silence.

Outside Khaled was manoeuvring the bus out of the parking bay. Maryam was waiting in the jeep with Yoko and two other trainees. She had to shout over the wind as we clambered in. "Sorry to drag

83

you guys out in this weather! There's so much to squeeze into the schedule as it is, we decided to chance it."

It was totally different to our dawn trip to Seshet. The river was utterly empty. Not even the brave little *feluccas* would risk coming out in this weather. On the road, we saw maybe five or six humans in total, all of them bent almost double against the wind, holding scarves across their faces as they hurried to find shelter.

We were five minutes from Seshet, when we heard a BANG like a bomb going off. I was looking in the wing mirror and I saw our back wheel suddenly trailing a smoking black rag behind it.

All the angel girls were screaming as the jeep went careering across the road. I was convinced we were going to turn over but Maryam was a star, quickly getting the vehicle back under control and switching off the engine.

"The tyre just blew out," she reassured us. "Is everyone OK back there?"

She sounded calm but we all knew tyres didn't just blow on celestial vehicles.

"I've got a spare," she told us, "but I don't think we should carry on. I'm going to call the hostel and get them to send someone out to pick us up."

We all settled down nervously to wait.

Lola knows me REALLY well, so she knew that breaking down in the desert wasn't my best thing.

She caught my eye and, as if we'd never quarrelled, she said perkily, "I spy with my little eye, something beginning with S."

"Very funny," I growled. "Sand."

"Correct!" She gave me a clap as if I was five. "Your turn!"

The wind's tense thrumming changed to an unearthly shriek. The jeep literally rocked on its tyres. Next minute the sandstorm came howling down from all sides.

The windscreen went yellow as a truckload of sand slammed into the jeep then went whirling away again. You can't believe how suffocating it feels inside a world of flying sand.

There was a moment of eerie stillness, then Yoko gave a squeal of fright. "Something's happening to the sand!"

The seething sand grains had started to swarm like angry hornets. We watched in horror as the swarms formed fast-moving spirals, circling ominously above our jeep like disembodied genies searching for a lamp.

"What *are* they?" Yoko quavered.

Before Maryam could answer the giant spirals morphed into huge figures. Suddenly we were surrounded by shrieking beast-headed beings.

Their unearthly screechy voices were worse than scraped metal, making us shrink down in our seats, clutching at our ears.

Like monstrous serpents their necks extended on and on, as the furious creatures stooped to flatten their faces against the windows, seeming to want to suck us in through their howling open mouths.

The angry gods in my exam nightmare had come to life.

"You said the gods were on our side!" I screamed at Maryam.

"Different gods!" she yelled. "The ancient Egyptians had a few Dark gods too."

With humungous tearing sounds, the jeep's canvas roof peeled back and went hurtling off into the storm.

A huge churning hole opened up in the sky over our heads.

"OMIGOSHHH!!!!!" Yoko wailed.

Lola made a grab for me just in time. Like fruit juice shooting up a straw, we were both sucked up helplessly into the raging cyclone, leaving the jeep like a little white speck far below.

We were yelling with terror, convinced we were going to get sucked right up into the sky hole and into a very bad place, but at the last minute there was a mighty SWOOSH, as a new unseen force blasted us in a totally different direction.

The Light gods had showed up finally, seeming determined not to let the Dark gods have things their own way.

Like a fraying rope in a cosmic tug of war, my soulmate and I were hauled this way and that by opposing divine forces.

Different types of lightning flashed and fizzled. Thunder rolled. I saw an absolutely spectacular lightning flash, which turned the sky into one vast crackling spider's web of light and suddenly my soulmate's hand was jerked right out of my grasp.

She was swept away screaming. I was screaming too. Seconds later there was a painful *thunk* as we smacked into each other again.

I made a frantic lunge, by some miracle grabbing hold of both her hands. "It's OK, sweetie, I've got you!" I yelled.

I was hurtling through the air at several hundred MPH as thunderbolts whistled past my ears, meanwhile being totally sandblasted by supernatural winds, plus my arms were half-wrenched out of their sockets. Yet, just like they tell you in those true life stories, I found the necessary strength to hang on to my best friend.

"If we stick together, we'll be OK!" I shrieked over the storm.

"Please don't drop me, Melanie!" she wailed.

I almost did – out of pure shock.

It wasn't Lola I'd saved. It was Maia!

CHAPTER NINE

Maybe the gods finally got what they wanted? I just know the sensation of enormous cosmic struggle magically stopped.

Maia and I went floating silently across the sky until, v. softly and gently, we were set down on the river bank in the syrupy gold light of late afternoon.

I knew we'd gone back in time. I knew the minute we touched the ground.

Ordinary sounds drifted through the evening air, the kind you can hear any day in almost any place on planet Earth. Little kids laughing, adults scolding, cocks crowing, the ring of hammers on metal.

I made myself turn around and it was true. The gods – who knew which ones? – had blown us back to ancient times. The lost city of Seshet was alive again!

A furious yell from Maia almost shocked me out of my skin.

"That was *not* part of my FREAKING plan." She flung her flip-flop across the sand in a temper. "'Oh, we'll be OK if we stick together'," she mimicked. "Well, we're freaking stuck together now!" And she turned her back on me as if this was all my fault.

Snatching off her cap, Maia pulled out a comb from somewhere and started angrily detangling her hair.

I have NO idea how our caps survived the storm, though Maia's had acquired interesting scorch marks from somewhere. One of those divine lightning bolts must have come a teensy bit too close.

Part of me was worrying about Lola, in case she'd been whirled off to some alien time-period all by herself. But deep down I sensed that wherever she was, she was OK. That's the thing with me and Lola – we might have fights, but we're always, *always* connected.

Since Maia was still ignoring me, I just sat in silence watching the sun go down over the Nile. I had no clue what time-period we'd landed in, but it had to be a long way from the mad, polluted century we'd just left. The atmosphere was so pure I felt like

I was literally swimming in the flaming oranges and golds of this old-style Egyptian sunset.

It was so peaceful after the horrendous chaos of the cosmic battle that I actually dozed off...

Something woke me, a tiny splash, a movement. Something.

I held my breath as a barge, ghostly in the twilight, came gliding into the bank.

I stumbled to my feet. For a moment I thought I must be dreaming, but it really was the same boat. I recognised the golden lotus flower gleaming on its prow.

We'd been blown back through human history just in time to see Cleopatra's barge arrive on its hush hush royal mission. Any minute now her messengers would be setting off to Seshet under cover of darkness in search of talented locals.

First the ancient gods of Egypt had shown me this event in a vision, now they'd whooshed us back to this moment for real. That suggested they had brought us here for a reason.

What was it Maryam said? Angels and gods only joined forces when something huge was at stake. Something like saving Queen Cleopatra and her country from the Romans maybe?

I was suddenly so wildly excited, I could hardly breathe.

I tapped Maia on the shoulder. "Babe, I think I know why we're here!"

CHAPTER TEN

"You really think we're here to help Cleopatra! We didn't just wash up here by accident?"

We were hurrying along in the shadow of the city wall, following Baraka, Adjo and the other courtiers from the royal barge.

Maia had snapped out of her sulk like magic as soon as I explained about seeing Cleopatra's barge in my vision. In fact she started squealing like an excited little girl!

"There's nothing accidental about this!" I assured her. "If you ask me, the gods, the friendly gods I mean, wanted us here all along. Khaled said when the gods have some little divine agenda going on, they give you, like, a teensy nudge."

"A teensy *nudge*!" Maia spluttered. "Is *that* what that was!"

"Not the sand storm, fluff-brain! That was the *Dark* gods!"

"Oops, I'm a bit confused," she giggled. "Who wants us to save Egypt again?"

"The good guys obviously," I said patiently, secretly enjoying my new role. It's usually Lola explaining everything to me!

"Wow, you have it all figured out," she grinned. "Good guys, bad guys. So where does a tragic cosmic dropout fit into this picture?"

I could have bitten off my tongue. I was so busy thinking of Maia as my angel colleague I'd totally forgotten her dark past.

She just laughed. "Relax, babe! I was only winding you up!"

When we reached the city gates, Baraka called out in a low voice. A shutter slid back and one of the courtiers passed something across with a chink of metal.

"Doesn't matter where you go, money always talks," Maia commented in my ear.

With stealthy grating sounds the watchman unbolted the gates, dragging them open just enough to let the men slip through.

They all hurried off to their designated areas.

"Which way?" Maia hissed.

Since she'd appointed me leader I said promptly, "Follow him!" meaning Baraka.

After a few minutes we emerged into a lively market place lit by burning torches. Market traders wrapped in woollen cloaks squatted on the ground beside heaps of local produce. One guy had baskets full of cheeping chicks so tiny they looked like balls of dandelion fluff.

Half-naked little kids were playing tag in the shadows, oblivious to the cold. I loved being able to understand all their joking and teasing. Understanding human languages is one of those angel freebies that always gives me a little buzz.

Baraka stopped to warm his hands over a street vendor's glowing brazier as he asked for directions. The man watched him walk away, sensing something unusual about this stranger.

There was a sudden commotion as a bunch of Roman soldiers came shambling into the marketplace looking, and smelling, like they'd fallen out of the nearest bar. People hastily pulled the little kids out of their way. One old man spat on the ground as the Romans staggered past, bawling out some crude army song.

Baraka just kept walking. You could feel him forcing himself not to look to see if he was being followed.

In the Street of Carpet Weavers, an animal smell of unwashed wool hung in the air mixed with deeply whiffy dye smells.

Baraka stopped outside one of the houses. A young man was sitting inside the doorway, peacefully looking up at the stars and sipping tea. Behind him I caught a glimpse of gorgeous textiles just bundled into casual heaps.

"I am sorry to disturb you," Baraka said politely, "but I have come to you on the queen's business."

The man gave an incredulous laugh. "I doubt that very much! I doubt the queen even knows I exist!"

A young woman came out, holding a naked baby boy in her arms. "No matter who's on the throne, they're always after your money!" she said good humouredly.

"Cleopatra's treasure houses are filled to bursting," the courtier reassured them. "She has no need of your money, but she does need your help."

"To do what?" asked the man obviously not convinced.

"To save Egypt," said Baraka very quietly.

I shot a thrilled glance at Maia.

Word of this exotic stranger's arrival spread just as Mardian had promised. In no time a small crowd was gathering outside the weaver's house, clearly thirsty for news of the outside world.

With no planes, phones or TV, it could take weeks before people in Seshet learned of events that were common knowledge hundreds of miles away in Alexandria. Everyone seemed to realise that Caesar's assassination had left Egypt vulnerable to Rome, but I don't think they'd grasped that their country was in imminent danger.

"It's just a matter of time before the Romans give the order to invade," Baraka told them gravely. "Our spies believe we have six months at most before their legions descend like locusts. But Queen Cleopatra has a plan!"

"I told you, she's after our gold!" The weaver's wife half-joked, to break the growing tension.

"In a way that's true!" Baraka gently touched her baby's perfect little forehead. "Our queen is after the precious hidden gold which lies inside each one of her people, the same golden qualities of ingenuity, patience and skill which brought Egypt to greatness long ago. Now Cleopatra asks you to pour out your hidden brilliance once again, to help her usher in a new and shining future for the Two Lands."

You could see people were genuinely moved.

"What would Cleopatra have us do?" someone asked Baraka.

"The actual details of our queen's plan are known only to Queen Cleopatra herself and her most trusted advisers. Even I may not be told what she intends to do. But she has sent us forth into her kingdom to search out the finest craftsmen and women in the land, and I know those who help her will be well rewarded."

"You did right to come to Seshet," an old man piped up. "We still keep to the old ways in Seshet."

I'd stopped listening. I may actually have stopped breathing.

I'd seen a girl in the crowd. She was clutching a bag of apricots to her chest. Tiny fruits kept spilling out, but she was too gripped by Baraka's speech to notice. I'd never seen her in my life, yet with a crazy leap of my heart, I recognised Sky Nolan.

CHAPTER ELEVEN

Maia refused to be impressed by this unexpected cosmic reunion.

"You only *want* to think it's her. How can you 'know' some totally random ancient Egyptian human is your old friend?"

"I just know, that's all," I said shakily. The extraordinary coincidence had shaken me to the core.

Baraka pulled an important looking scroll from inside his cloak, and started to read from a list of skills and talents which were apparently crucial to Cleopatra's mysterious plan. "Glassblowers, carpenters..."

I moved in closer to this strange yet fabulously familiar version of my friend, and realised for the first time that her clothes were almost threadbare. It was the proud way she carried herself that made you not notice at first. She had fastened a fresh lotus blossom in her glossy black hair. She had attitude, like my Sky. And like Sky, she was lonely to her bones.

"Dancers, acrobats, silk weavers," Baraka was reeling off.

In a rush of cosmic info I knew everything about this girl's life. Her dad was dangerously ill. He hadn't taken solid food for days, but tonight he'd had a sudden longing for apricots. She'd dashed to the market to buy some, but something about this stranger from Alexandria had stopped her in her tracks.

"Linen weavers, jewellers, perfume blenders..."

I saw sudden longing in her face.

"Shame," someone muttered behind her. "Her father ran the finest perfume business in Upper Egypt before he married that witch."

The girl who was, or one day would be, Sky, whirled around. "My father's not dead yet," she flashed back. "So don't talk about him as if he's already gone to the Field of Reeds!"

Another girl was watching her with concern. Like my friend, she was underfed and poorly dressed.

She tentatively touched her arm. "How is he, Khamsin?"

"Why should you care, Amisi?" she snapped. "Your uncle and aunt are just waiting for him to die so they can steal his customers!"

"I know and it makes me feel ashamed," Amisi said huskily. "Your father has always been kind to me. It's a pity he chose a bad wife."

Khamsin's face showed absolutely no emotion. "It's not hard to fool a man with a motherless child!"

An old woman came half-running into the street, weeping as she ran. "He's calling for you, Khamsin!"

Apricots rolled everywhere as Khamsin dropped her bag and ran, literally pushing people out of her way.

"I've got to go with her," I told Maia. "You can tell me what happens."

"Gosh, I'm all confused!" she said brightly. "Weren't we saving Egypt a few minutes ago?"

She was obviously hopping mad that I was taking off without her, but just now saving Egypt suddenly seemed far less important than supporting this human girl, a girl I couldn't help thinking of as my friend.

Khamsin lived just round the corner in the Street of Perfume Blenders, and I don't think there has ever been a sweeter smelling street on Earth. As for her actual house, it literally smelled like paradise. As Khamsin opened the door, thousands of delicious scents, floral, musky, subtle, spicy, came swimming in through my senses.

In the front room, a few reed lamps gave a smoky glimmer, enough for a rushed impression of carved cabinets and softly gleaming bottles, as we pelted through.

Khamsin's dad seemed well-off for these times. *Why doesn't he buy his daughter some new clothes?* I wondered.

Then I remembered that Khamsin had a step-mother.

Male and female laughter floated down from an upstairs room. I could hear sharp clicking sounds, like counters being slammed down, and shouts of "Cheat!" Khamsin's step-mum had invited her mates round to play board games, the way you do when your husband is dying.

Khamsin didn't even glance in their direction. She flew through the back of the house and out again into a starlit courtyard.

A flight of stone steps went up to the Egyptian-style flat roof. Khamsin took them in a stumbling rush.

"He says he can't go, dearie, not till he tells you what's on his mind," the old woman wheezed behind her.

Khamsin's father was lying under a heap of furs and blankets, but his teeth were chattering with cold. Beads of sweat stood out on his papery yellow skin. He was obviously in terrible pain.

"Isis help him," Khamsin whispered. "Help us both."

Then she ran to him and took both his hands.

When humans are dying, they sometimes need to set the record straight before they leave their bodies forever. Khamsin's dad had obviously been torturing himself over something he should have told his daughter long ago.

"Your mother wanted... give it... to you," he gasped out." But I said... too dangerous for such a young—"

"He's been like this since you left," the old woman explained as if the poor man was deaf.

Khamsin's father was mumbling feverishly. "Had to swear... secret... handed down from mother to—"

He gave a groan as the pain stabbed again deep inside.

When he could speak again he seemed to have lost his thread. "...rats... couldn't read half... but your mother... determined to—"

Suddenly the dying man's eyes filled with a kind of exhausted happiness. Every cell in my body tingled as a precious memory shimmered from his mind into mine.

I saw his dark-haired young wife, as if I was watching with him through an open door. Surrounded by exotic plant materials and scribbled notes in Egyptian hieroglyphics, she was dripping a silvery-green essence into a tiny glass vial.

"Best perfume blender in the Two Lands... and most beautiful" he murmured. "Stubborn too... worked through the night... till she... found... secret of Nefertiti's perfume—"

I almost bit through my lip.

I know what some people would say. Khamsin's dad was dying an excruciatingly painful death. To make his agonies more bearable, he had escaped into an Egyptian fairy tale where his young wife had rediscovered the secret formula for Nefertiti's perfume.

I can only say it didn't seem like that to Khamsin. I saw her blink with shock as she took in what he was saying.

He struggled to sit up. "You know… where I keep the frankincense?"

Khamsin sounded as if she was talking in her sleep. "In the big chest. You never let anyone go to that drawer, even me."

"Your step-mother mustn't—" He fell back again, groaning. "Should never have—" he told someone Khamsin couldn't see. "But a girl needs a mother—"

I gave a little gasp of surprise. He was talking to me.

If he was seeing angels, he probably didn't have much longer.

"You did the best you could," I told him softly. "Don't feel bad. I'll take care of Khamsin for you, I promise."

Khamsin was so pale I thought she was going to faint. "You mustn't talk, Father, just rest."

His eyes went back to Khamsin. He gave her a look filled with so much love it made my heart feel too way big for my chest. "You're just as lovely as your mother," he mumbled.

They were his last words.

Khamsin never took her eyes off his face as the gap between those terrible rasping breaths grew longer.

I didn't see the goddess come to take his spirit away to the Field of Reeds. I just felt my bare arms break into goose bumps as a tingly breeze came sweeping across the roof, and suddenly it was over.

Khamsin let out a heart-rending howl then she threw herself across her father's body, shuddering with silent sobs.

Her step-mother came hurrying up to the roof with several curious friends and relatives. She was younger than I'd imagined, perhaps only eight or nine years older than Khamsin. Like a lot of humans who get too close to the PODS, her eyes had almost no expression. She bent over her husband's corpse. For a surprised moment I thought she was going to kiss him. Actually she was just checking he was really dead.

"At last," she said in a bored voice. "I thought the old fool would never go."

Chapter Twelve

Khamsin's relations lifted her father's corpse on to a stretcher and carried it out of the house.

I could hear them going down the street, howling and wailing in a display of totally fake emotion.

The old woman hovered, saying the usual things. Khamsin's dad's troubles were over. He was going to be reunited with his wife in the Field of Reeds. Eventually she left. Then Khamsin lay down on the roof and cried until I thought she'd make herself sick.

After a few minutes, I felt a strangely familiar vibe. For a moment I actually wondered if there was another angel in the area.

I heard a husky mew, and glanced up in time to see a small skinny cat bound across the narrow gap between Khamsin's house and next door's roof.

Like the kitty Lola rescued at the temple, this one had cute tufty ears and spotted markings. She came straight to me first, making the most hilarious little squeaks, like she'd been looking for me all around Seshet and was incredibly excited to have tracked me down finally. I knew she was really just attracted to my cosmic vibes.

Next she trotted over to Khamsin and started purring like a small generator, rubbing her head lovingly against her cheek.

I remembered the way my nan's cat would make a fuss of me when I was upset. It always helped, like it was helping Khamsin now.

Gradually her sobs quietened down.

I don't know how long we stayed like that – long enough to see three shooting stars streak down silently through the dark.

Cleopatra's messengers had probably gone back to their barge by this time. Maia would be hanging around the market place impatiently waiting for me to come back. To be honest I didn't give her much thought. I was concentrating all my energies on Khamsin, talking to her softly, reminding her she had an entire cosmic agency looking out for her, in addition to her local gods.

I was hoping to avoid a rerun, you see, of what happened to Sky. She'd been hurt just one too many times. Her dad walking out, her mum going nuts, then her best friend getting knocked down by a hit and run driver – it was too much for a vulnerable thirteen-year-old to take.

No wonder she gave up on herself, just like the PODS had been hoping.

Would Khamsin give up on herself now she'd lost her only loving parent? Afraid to know the answer, I just kept talking, trusting that my spangly new birthday vibes were getting through.

A fourth shooting star shot down from the heavens. This time I shivered. The Universe is full of these huge glittering comings and goings, but did anyone have the slightest idea what any of it actually meant?

I heard a rustle as Khamsin dragged herself into a sitting position. She looked around her in a daze, seeming amazed to find her world still in one piece. The kitty jumped up on her lap and Khamsin absently stroked her without thinking.

A zillion lovely scents wafted up to us from the Street of Perfume Blenders.

"Omigosh," I breathed. "How stupid am I?"

"I'm *working* on *a really special perfume counter.*" That's what Sky said in my dream. And Khamsin, who was really Sky in ancient-Egyptian-style packaging, was a perfume blender's daughter!

I hadn't been able to help my friend in my own time, but it seemed like the gods wanted me to have another chance.

"If I'd known this all happened to her before, I'd have understood Sky much better," I told the cat softly. "She could be *such* a diva, but deep down she was just terrified of being left alone."

The kitty's glowing almond-shaped eyes were so sympathetic, it was almost like she understood what I was saying.

A new thought nudged into my mind. "You're right," I whispered, as if we were really having a conversation. "Human history just *seems* to flow in a straight line, but really it happens all at once. Maybe Khamsin's Egyptian life isn't 'before' her life as Sky? Maybe – omigosh – maybe, both lives are going on at the same time? And maybe, if I could help Khamsin get herself sorted in this life, it might have a knock-on effect, and Sky would..."

With an angry hiss, the kitty jumped off Khamsin's lap.

Maia appeared at the top of the steps. "You're not *still* here!" she said accusingly.

"I had to stay," I explained. "Her dad just died."

She plumped herself down beside me. "I heard. Murdered if you believe the rumours. They're saying his wife poisoned him so she could move her Roman boyfriend in."

Poison. No wonder Khamsin's dad died in such agony.

"They reckon Khamsin's next on her hit list," Maia added coolly as if she was commenting on the weather.

"You're kidding!" I gasped. It hadn't occurred to me that Khamsin was in actual physical danger as well as everything else. "If everyone *knows*, why don't they report her?"

"Too scared!" grinned Maia. "She was a herbalist before she married and it seems she's a *leetle* bit too interested in the dark side of her profession!"

Just at that moment Maia reminded me of Brice in his bad boy days. Maybe they'd seen so much horror in the Dark dimensions that one little murder more or less didn't really register?

Maia let out a giggle. "I should really be a spy. It's amazing what you find out! Apparently one of

Khamsin's mum's ancestors actually created a secret perfume for some famous queen."

"Nefertiti," I whispered. "The most beautiful woman in history."

Maia seemed disappointed. "I'm surprised you heard. No one spoke about it even inside the family. The way they talked in the market, you'd think the perfume was magic, literally!"

"No man could refuse her anything when she wore it," I said softly. "Khamsin's mum inherited the recipe and dedicated her life to recreating it."

Maia's eyes narrowed. "You *have* been doing your homework! But Khamsin's dad never told anyone about his wife's amazing achievement. He thought if it got out someone might kill both him and Khamsin to get their hands on the secret papyrus!"

I shook my head. "That's so sad. Khamsin's step-mum never even knew about it but she killed him just the same."

As if she'd heard, Khamsin suddenly jumped up. "I'm not sticking around to be her next victim," she said aloud. "Queen Cleopatra didn't sit around waiting for her enemies to murder her. I'm going to Alexandria to seek my fortune."

And she went rushing off down the steps.

I couldn't believe what had just happened! I'd spent DAYS trying to get through to Sky. Khamsin had turned her life around in *minutes*.

I felt the little cat brush past my ankles as we followed Khamsin back into the house.

Her bedroom was just an alcove, with an old curtain pulled across. She threw a few clothes into a basket and I thought she was going to fly straight out of the house.

Instead she grabbed one of the lamps, using the feeble light to help her select several tiny bottles from the perfume blending room, hastily stowing them in her bag. Next Khamsin ran her eyes along a cluttered work bench, swooping on various perfume making implements, including a dropper.

Finally she fished something down from the lintel above the workroom door. The key to the chest.

Almost as tall as Khamsin, the chest was divided into shallow drawers. Each drawer had its own keyhole above a label in faded red-painted hieroglyphics.

Khamsin unlocked one of the drawers and slid it open, releasing an earthy yet deeply soulful scent. I'd smelled frankincense before in Nero's Rome, and I knew that in ancient times this sweet-smelling resin was almost as precious as rubies.

Khamsin's hands shook as she removed the flat ebony box from the drawer and dropped it into her bag. The slightest sound from the street outside made her jump, but she controlled her trembling as she carefully lifted out the papyrus.

She unrolled a few centimetres and got a surprise. There were *two* scrolls: a newer papyrus concealing the fragile yellowing one inside. Khamsin caught her breath as she saw the hieroglyphics at the top of the outer scroll, the notes her mum had scribbled on her experiments.

Khamsin's breathing was genuinely panicky now. This was all taking too long. What if they came back and caught her trying to run away? She frantically unfastened her belt, pulled up her dress and quickly concealed the scrolls next to her skin, retying her belt tightly to keep them in place.

"Naughty girly," murmured Maia.

"It's not stealing," I said defensively. "Her parents *wanted* her to have them."

"She's a bright cookie anyway. If Queen Cleopatra is serious about bringing Egypt into a new golden age, having Nefertiti's perfume would give her a head start."

My mouth dropped open. "I thought Khamsin wanted those scrolls because they were her mum's!"

"Wake up sweetie! If that *is* Nefertiti's perfume recipe she's just stuffed up her jumper, little Cinders here has got herself a meal ticket for life!"

I can be so dumb. When Khamsin said she was going to seek her fortune, she *totally* meant it!

Maia gave me a playful poke in the ribs. "That's the problem with angel schools. They teach all this wussy stuff about love and light. In Hell school they're more into evil motives and strategies!"

Khamsin opened the front door a crack, glancing nervously up the street. The little cat rubbed against her ankles mewing anxiously. Suddenly Khamsin scooped the kitty up and popped it into her basket.

"She's never taking the cat!" Maia sounded appalled.

The kitty immediately made herself at home among Khamsin's clothes, treading and kneading with her paws, like, OK, it's a little cramped but I can work with this!

Maia peered at me astonished. "Are you smiling or crying?"

I didn't even know myself. I just knew that before the PODS got into her head, my Sky would have taken the kitty too.

CHAPTER THIRTEEN

I don't know *how* Khamsin knew where she was going! All the streets were pitch black, except for the odd glimmery window.

Maia puffed out her cheeks as we hurried along. "So what's the new game plan?"

"Well, we have to keep Khamsin safe," I said, just stopping myself from adding, "Obviously."

"Seems a bit random," she objected. "Safe from what exactly?"

"From her psycho step-mum for starters! Also any unsavoury cosmic influences that might decide to take advantage while she's in such a vulnerable space."

Maia laughed, though I didn't think I'd said anything funny.

"So we're babysitting her basically," she said in a sneering voice. "And how long do you plan on keeping this up?"'

I tried to imagine Lola asking how long we'd have to take care of a needy human. But being snotty with Maia wasn't going to improve her rusty angel skills. Tact and encouragement were what she needed.

"It takes as long as it takes, babe," I said as gently as I could. "This is a dangerous—"

"—time for her, yeah, I got that. Personally I preferred Plan A: Saving Cleo. Way more high profile."

I saw Maia's teeth flash in the dark as she let out another of her random giggles. "You should see your face! You thought I was serious!" She hooked her arm through mine." We'll beat off those Evil Bean Pods, sweetie, don't you worry!"

Khamsin reached the gates just as the watchman was urgently shepherding the last volunteers out of the city. Some people were leading pack mules, their hooves muffled with old rags. They looked nervous but secretly proud of themselves at the same time. This morning they'd been weaving coloured threads, or pouring white-hot metal into moulds, never dreaming that tonight they'd be setting off on a dangerous adventure to save queen and country.

"Hurry if you're coming, Miss!" the watchman called hoarsely to Khamsin, obviously terrified someone would shop him to the Romans.

The gates were closing behind us when someone shrieked "WAIT!" A girl squeezed through an almost non-existent gap.

"Amisi!" gasped Khamsin.

It was too dark to see Amisi clearly, but I knew immediately what had happened. Violence doesn't only leave bruises and broken bones, it leaves a really ugly vibe.

Seeing her grand plan going out the window, Khamsin was too freaked to notice. She dragged Amisi out of earshot. "This isn't going to work," she hissed. "They won't take two perfume blenders from one town."

Amisi sounded pitiful. "I know, I wouldn't have come. I just thought, with your dad—"

"He's dead," Khamsin told her bleakly. "I'm supposed to be next."

Amisi gave a gasp. "Oh Khamsin."

Suddenly both girls were holding on to each other, weeping.

At last Amisi let her go, giving her a little push. "Hurry or they'll leave you behind. I'll pray to Isis to keep you safe."

Khamsin hovered, clearly unsure about leaving Amisi outside the city walls. "But they won't let you back in now till morning."

"I don't mind. It's peaceful out here. Have a good life, Khamsin." Amisi couldn't quite manage to hide her tears.

Khamsin suddenly peered into her face. I heard her suck in her breath. "Who's been hitting you?"

"My uncle." Amisi whispered, instinctively covering her damaged eye. "I can't go back there, Khamsin, I can't!"

"No, because I won't let you," said Khamsin grimly. "What else can you do apart from blend perfumes?"

"I can charm snakes," offered Amisi. She managed a wan smile. "It's a family thing. My granny could do it."

Khamsin frowned. "Snake charmers weren't on the list." I could feel her mind working overtime. "They need dancers. Can you dance?"

Amisi sounded ashamed. "Like a hippo my uncle says. Perfume and snakes – that's all I know."

119

Khamsin took a deep breath. "Perfume blending it is then."

"But you said they wouldn't take—?"

Khamsin just linked arms with Amisi as if everything was settled. "I'm assuming we won't have to *walk* all the way to Alexandria to find out what our queen is up to?" she said with a tired grin. "I left before her messenger got to the travel arrangements part."

Visibly stunned by Khamsin's turn around, Amisi was trying not to cry.

"A mule caravan leaves tonight," she gulped. "But we have to see someone called Mardian first. If he doesn't choose us, we'll have to go back."

"He'll choose us, don't worry," said Khamsin fiercely.

Maia made a rude noise. "How random is this girl? Weighing herself down with stray kittens and lame ducks. She'd better not be planning to share Nefertiti's secret recipe with Amisi, that's all I can say!"

I'd had to stop to blow my nose. I couldn't believe how lovely Khamsin was being, on what surely must seem like the worst night of her life. "Why would that be so wrong?" I sniffled.

"Hello! This is Khamsin's chance to make it big! Not too sensible to just hand it all over to the first human with a hard luck story!"

I opened my mouth and immediately shut it again.

Maia gave a deep sigh. "Oh bum! Is this one of those love 'n light things that a rubbish angel like me couldn't possibly understand?"

I gave a splutter of surprised laughter through my tears. "Kind of," I admitted.

On second thoughts I decided Maia wasn't doing so badly. Brice was back from the Hell dimensions ages before he could crack dark angel jokes.

We'd arrived back at Cleopatra's barge.

Adjo was ushering people on to the boat in ones and twos. The rest waited their turn, talking quietly.

"She's not like those other Ptolemies," said a young silversmith. "Couldn't be bothered to learn two words of our language most of them. Never set foot outside that big white palace, so I heard!"

"Imagine that sweet young girl growing up in that nest of vipers," tisked someone. "Didn't one of her brothers try to have her killed?"

"Her own sister plotted against her," said the silversmith grimly. "But she was a match for all of them. I don't care if her ancestors were from Macedonia or they came from the moon, Cleopatra has an Egyptian heart. If anyone can make Egypt great again, she can!"

At last it was Khamsin and Amisi's turn to follow Adjo across the plank. He led them into the circle of torch-light where Mardian waited to meet them. Neither of them looked much like potential royal perfumers, I have to say.

Mardian wore an immense gold collar with his gorgeous robes, a sign of his v. important status at Cleopatra's court, I found out later. He sat smiling and patient in his high-backed chair, also made of solid gold, even though I could tell he was secretly longing for his bed.

Beside him sat one of the most elegant young women I'd ever seen. Except that it was long and flowing, I don't remember what she was wearing I just remember her jewels, a simple circle of pearls fastened around her brow, glimmering softly against her ebony skin.

Baraka introduced her as Lady Iras, the queen's lady in waiting. Amisi looked ready to faint. If these godlike beings just *worked* for Cleopatra, what must the queen be like!!

When Mardian asked what two such young girls were doing on the wrong side of the city wall in the middle of the night, Khamsin flashed, "On the queen's business same as you, sir. My friend and I risked our lives to bring her majesty something of great importance and – *antiquity*," she pronounced carefully.

"Very well," he sighed. "Show me your ancient relic."

Khamsin backed out of reach. "I can't do that sir."

He looked astounded. "Dear child, do you think I would *steal* it?"

"I'm sorry, sir," she said firmly. "This is all I – *we* have – to make our way in the world. It's for the queen's eyes only, sir."

Mardian's eyebrows shot up. "You *do* think I'd steal it!"

"Child, you go too far," Adjo said through clenched teeth.

"I'm sorry sir, but it does happen, sir," Khamsin said stubbornly.

Lady Iras leaned forward. "This offering must be something very precious. May we at least know what it is?"

123

Khamsin nodded, relieved. "Oh yes please, madam."

She explained as quickly as possible about the royal perfume recipe passed from mother to daughter for over a thousand years.

Mardian gave an involuntary glance into the darkness, where volunteers still waited to be interviewed. "An intriguing tale," he said politely. "And I sympathise with your dilemma, but if you won't show us, how do we know you're telling the truth?"

"Ho-ho, a stand-off," Maia giggled in my ear.

Amisi whispered, "Show them, Khamsin, just don't let them touch it."

"They could just grab it!" Khamsin hissed.

"They won't. They work for *her*," Amisi whispered back.

"All right," Khamsin agreed unhappily. She untied her belt, and after a short struggle managed to extract the scrolls, while the VIPs politely looked away. Khamsin unrolled a few inches of papyrus and nervously held it up.

Mardian glanced, not too hopefully, at the scroll then I saw his expression change. "More light!" he bellowed.

A slave hurried over with a fresh torch.

Mardian abruptly switched from Egyptian to Greek. "I actually believe it's genuine. This is definitely Nefertiti's cartouche!" He gave a dubious glance at the girls. "Do you think they stole it?"

Khamsin suddenly interrupted, also in Greek, to their obvious surprise. "I speak six languages and I can understand every word you say."

Mardian tried to interrupt but she rushed on.

"I am not some little girl making flower petal perfume for her dollies. All my ancestors were perfume blenders. Perfume making runs in my blood. I can identify six different varieties of *rose absolute* blindfolded. I know how to use essences to lift a mood or calm a racing mind. While my father lay ill, I haggled with his traders for him, *and* I took over blending the incense for the temple. THREE different kinds, sir, for three different times of day – and nobody guessed I did it and not my father."

"I'm not quite sure what you're saying," said Mardian, obviously taken aback.

"I am saying we did not steal it sir," said Khamsin bravely. "It was my mother's wish that I should inherit it."

Mardian and Iras had a murmured conversation. Lady Iras turned to Khamsin. "How is your father now?'

"He died just tonight, madam." Khamsin only just managed to keep her voice from shaking.

"And how old are you, my dears?' asked Lady Iras.

"I am thirteen," said Khamsin.

"Twelve and a half," whispered Amisi, twisting her hands in her skirt.

"And is perfume blending in your blood too?" Lady Iras asked Amisi.

"Yes, madam." Her voice was almost inaudible.

Mardian and Lady Iras briefly conferred again.

"If we take you, will you both do your utmost to recreate this perfume for the queen?" Mardian asked them in his dry tone.

They nodded eagerly.

"And no one will come after us accusing us of child-stealing?"

Khamsin's face was stony. "My step-mother and her boyfriend will be happy to see me go."

"And will your unusually silent friend's family be happy to see her go?"

That little kitty had the *best* cosmic timing! She suddenly poked her head out of Khamsin's basket with a friendly 'Pirrip!', like, "*Hi, you starry VIPs!*"

Lady Iras burst into delighted laughter.

Mardian beckoned to Baraka. "We will take a gamble on these young criminals," he said, chuckling. "I'm not so sure about their accomplice! From the way she is scratching, I suspect she has fleas."

Khamsin shook her head. "She has to come. The gods sent her to me."

Mardian and Lady Iras seemed to think this was a perfectly normal thing to say. "When the gods send gifts, only a fool turns them away," Lady Iras agreed.

"Find somewhere for them to sleep," Mardian told Baraka. "Clear a storeroom if need be."

Baraka seemed startled. "You intend them to travel with us, my lord?"

Mardian stifled a yawn. "The papyrus has survived for over one thousand eight hundred years. It would be a shame to lose it to bandits now, don't you think?"

"He's such a sweetie," I whispered to Maia. "He feels genuinely protective towards those girls."

"I doubt it. Humans usually turn out to have a secret agenda."

"Maia!" I protested.

She giggled. "Oops – was my dark side showing again!"

"Just a bit!"

I couldn't help laughing. Maia was outrageous sometimes.

I heard Baraka teasing the girls as they stumbled sleepily below decks. "It's ten days or more to Alexandria by river. If you haven't come up with the goods by then we'll just have to throw you to the crocodiles."

"Do you see how the Universe works!" I wanted to tell Maia. "We went with the flow, and it still panned out!" Not only were we still on track for saving Egypt, we were going to do it in luxury!

But no one likes to hear, "I told you so." Plus if we were going to be stuck on the same boat for ten days, we had heaps of time to work on Maia's attitude.

CHAPTER FOURTEEN

I could feel the river flying past in my sleep as Cleopatra's barge travelled through what was left of the night. Tomorrow we'd stop at Abydos, the next town along the Nile, where Mardian and his team would rope in another batch of gifted humans for the queen's mystery project. Before he left the girls to settle for the night, Baraka had reeled off the names of the other towns where we'd be stopping over on our journey; Hermopolis, Heliopolis, Memphis, Saqqara, Giza with its famous pyramids...

I vaguely heard Maia leave the cabin in the early hours, muttering about a headache and fresh air.

The next thing I knew, I felt a light dab on my cheek. I opened my eyes to see Khamsin's cat gazing intensely into my face. When she saw I was awake she started washing, tail-tip twitching, obviously alert to every tiny sound, like, *Don't let your guard down, angel girl. You lucked out with the royal barge, but these are dangerous times.*

"I don't know, kitty!" I teased her. "Divine cats are soo bossy!"

I was just playing. I knew the cat wasn't really talking to me.

A woman slave softly entered the cabin with a jug of scented hot water. Another slave followed with an armful of freshly ironed clothes. The slaves left as silently as they came, but they had somehow changed the vibe in the cabin and Khamsin and Amisi sleepily opened their eyes.

I wish you'd seen their faces as they took in the full gorgeousness of their accommodation for the first time – the carved furniture made from exotic scented wood, the richly coloured rugs and hangings.

Amisi pulled the sheet over her head and I heard a muffled wail. "I want to stay in this dream forever!"

A male slave stole in with a tray laden with fruits and preserves, and a stack of warm flat bread wrapped in a snowy cloth.

When he'd gone, Amisi slipped out of bed and

tiptoed to the tray. I heard her stomach growl. "Khamsin," she hissed. "This tray is made of *gold*!"

"Don't touch the food!" Khamsin said fiercely.

Amisi looked bewildered.

"The gods gave us a new life! We've got to do things right. We'll wash and put on clean clothes first, then we'll eat."

And Amisi humbly agreed.

I don't know if it was gratitude to the gods, or if Baraka's crocodile joke had stuck in Khamsin's mind, but after a huge breakfast, she unpacked her perfume-making tools and she and Amisi set to work.

They immediately hit a snag. A glance at Khamsin's mum's notes showed her she was missing crucial ingredients.

Khamsin tugged at her hair. "We need some costus before we can even get started. They used that a lot in the old days as a base."

"Khamsin, I have some!" Unwrapping her cloth bundle, Amisi tipped out several small bottles, pushing one across to Khamsin. "I thought they owed me," she said, seeing Khamsin's surprise, and her hand crept up to cover her swollen eye.

When Khamsin removed the stopper from Amisi's bottle, the kitty backed off in alarm. I thought 'costus' smelled like an extremely confusing cross between damp violets (*mmm*) and damp dog hair (*euw!*).

"It's good stuff," Khamsin pronounced.

As I listened to them talking, I realised that blending perfumes was a bit like chemistry. Used in micro-quantities, in combination with certain other ingredients, this bizarre wet dog/violets combo would be changed into something rich and warm.

I thought you could just bung all the smells in one bottle, shake it up and bingo – perfume! But with really special perfumes apparently, you had to take it slow, leaving certain smells to 'marry' with each other, keeping your blend warm or cool depending. I started wondering if ten days was going to be enough!

But as Khamsin and Amisi went on enthusiastically swapping info, it dawned on me that ancient Egyptian-style perfume making was also very much like magic. For instance at one crucial stage in the perfume making process, you had to repeat certain charms, plus at the proper time you exposed your blend to starlight or moonlight, so as to absorb divine vibes from Nut, the goddess of the sky.

It turned out that between them the girls had almost two thirds of the ingredients on Khamsin's mum's list. The rest they could pick up along the way.

Amisi said her uncle didn't give two figs about perfume, he just sold the stuff. Khamsin said viciously that her step-mum couldn't tell frankincense from mule dung which made Amisi laugh.

"Khamsin isn't an Egyptian name," she commented curiously.

Khamsin looked faintly embarrassed. "It's what desert dwellers call the wind that brings storms. The *khamsin* was blowing when I was born."

That girl was destined to have a cosmic name whenever, I thought. *Sky, wind...*

"My name means flower," said Amisi. I could see she half-expected Khamsin to laugh.

"Obviously the gods always intended you to be a perfume blender," Khamsin said, with one of her rare smiles.

Amisi turned away. She wasn't used to hearing positive things about herself.

Lady Iras popped her head round the door, smiling to see the girls with their tiny bottles of oils and essences lined up on the rug. "Mardian sent me to tell you not to spend all day sweltering below

133

decks," she said firmly. "You have to come up and see your beautiful land!"

Like the queen, Lady Iras wasn't technically Egyptian. I'd heard the girls say she was from Nubia. Yet like Cleopatra, she was totally Egyptian in her heart.

I followed them up on deck, wanting to see if Maia was OK.

It was a truly lovely morning. Birds were darting everywhere. A heron was standing on one long thin leg among the reeds like it was doing yoga practice. White lotus flowers floated on the water.

Maia was sitting with her eyes closed, listening to her iPod and looking like death. I touched her on the knee.

"Oh hi," she said listlessly, taking off her head phones.

"Not feeling too good?"

She shook her head.

"Oh no!" I exclaimed "When did you lose your pendant?"

"Oh, I lost it in the storm," she said without much interest.

I gasped to see the livid burn mark where her ankh had been.

"Some of that divine lightning must have hit you! No wonder you feel rough. It's weird you didn't get symptoms till now though."

"I know," said Maia feebly. "I think the smell of Khamsin's oils pushed me over the edge. I might have to stay up on deck from now on. Sorry babe, I know I'm leaving you to do all the hard work."

"Khamsin and Amisi aren't exactly hard work!" I said to reassure her. It wasn't how I'd imagined this trip working out, but Maia couldn't help being under the weather. That's what I told myself, and if I had doubts, I quickly pushed them out of sight.

Chapter Fifteen

My days slipped into a pattern, as I kept busy going back and forth between the girls and my invalid friend.

We were gradually leaving the arid land of Upper Egypt behind. The air became more humid and different plants grew on the lush green banks. One morning we saw a family of hippos dozing among the reeds, like small, half-submerged mountains. It was the first time I'd realised why Egyptians called their country the Two Lands. It really did feel like we were gliding through a different world.

Maia stayed up on deck as we'd agreed, but she still had vague flu symptoms, which she insisted was down to the divine lightning burn.

One night I came up to give her a progress report on the girls.

"I can't believe how well they're getting on! Sky never let anyone get close. Khamsin's been hurt too but she's willing to risk making friends."

"Yeah well, early days," Maia said grimly. "Wasn't Sky mixed up with the – what do your mates call the Dark agencies? Pea pods?"

"No pea, just PODS," I corrected, embarrassed for some reason.

Despite her aches and pains, Maia seemed tickled. "Oh, like shorthand for Powers of Darkness. *Très* sinister!"

"It was Sky's boyfriend who was in with them, anyway, not Sky," I objected. "He's nothing to do with Khamsin."

She shrugged. "Once humans get into a groove, they tend to stay there for life after life."

I was shocked. "I don't agree! If angels don't believe people are basically good, what the sassafras are we *for*?"

Maia quickly looked away. Even by the flickery torch-light I could see she was too pale. I felt ashamed of myself for almost shouting at a sick angel girl.

She said humbly, "You care about these kids, don't you? I could learn a lot from you." I didn't know what to say, so I hastily changed the subject.

"I can't wait to find out about Cleopatra's plan, can you?" I giggled. "I can't imagine how she's going to defeat the Romans with a bunch of silversmiths and pastry chefs and whatever. It sounds almost like she's planning some seriously upscale party."

I didn't know it, but I wasn't actually that far off.

The kitty had followed me up on deck. Now Adjo was gently scratching her around the ears, which made her purr with pleasure.

"You have the eyes of the moon goddess," he told her. "You will bring us luck."

"There is something special about that cat," I said to Maia. "You know she appeared, like, *minutes* after Khamsin's dad died?"

Maia shuddered. "Ugh! Cats creep me out." She saw my shocked expression and groaned. "You love them, right?"

"I thought all angels liked animals," I admitted.

She sighed. "Actually, it's more that cats don't like me. She won't come near me, haven't you noticed? And she watches me all the time."

This was true, I realised. I remembered how the cat had hissed a warning, just before Maia appeared on the roof. I wasn't about to read anything sinister into that. Everyone knows animals have sharp senses. She must have picked up a teeny whiff of Hell residue on Maia. Brice's jacket still smells whiffy though he's been back ages now.

Maia wrapped her arms round herself, shivering. "Sometimes I think I've gone too far to go back now," she said bleakly.

"You *are* back, you silly angel girl," I teased, trying to make her smile. "Everything is going to get better and better now, you'll see. Seriously, I've seen it happen with Brice."

I was bewildered to see Maia's eyes fill with tears. Even after everything that happened later, I still think those tears were real.

I woke up next morning with a mission.

I was going to help this troubled angel girl rebuild her shattered confidence. Maia just needed someone to believe in her, the way Lola had believed in Brice. Brice was easily as bad as Maia when we first met him, if not worse – and look at him now!

I felt a burst of happiness radiating from my heart, like a tiny sun. With my support, Maia was going to blossom into a really special angel – maybe more special than most, because she'd been into the dark and come back.

I flew up on deck to share my early morning thoughts, but there was no sign of Maia anywhere, it was like she'd just dropped off the boat.

Really this is a good sign, I told myself quickly. If she's gone for a walk, she's getting better.

The previous night we had moored close to a temple where the priests were friendly to Cleopatra's cause. The scent of almond blossom from the temple orchards wafted through the boat. It was so early only slaves and angels were awake.

I went to dangle my legs over the water. Morning mists were rising from the river bank. It was nice, like being in your own private scented sauna!

I heard a familiar giggle and Maia materialised beside me. "Sorry babe, had to get away for a few minutes! Can't take being stuck in one place."

I thought Maia had been gone much longer than a few minutes, but she looked like a different angel girl. She was absolutely glowing.

"I used to be like that," I admitted. "Reuben used to call me Houdini. I just hated being pinned down!

Couldn't work in a team, couldn't keep to a timetable!"

Maia gave me a sly smirk. "Is Reuben your boyfriend?"

"No! He's just a really good friend who happens to be a boy."

"Yeah, yeah! So where does poor Indigo fit into all this?"

I tossed my hair, secretly enjoying Maia's version of me as a heavenly sexpot. "Hey keep your options open, I say!"

"So you won't mind if I go walkabout now and again?"

"Of course not."

Maia flashed me one of her fabulous smiles. "You could come with me!" she offered. "I found this really cool little oasis."

"One of us has to stay with the girls," I said firmly.

She pouted like a little kid. "Surely you can leave them for half an hour? What could happen in half an hour?"

"Maia! The gods blew us back to Cleopatra's time to take care of them! They must have *some* concerns about their safety."

Her expression darkened. "Sometimes you are

too freaking angelly for words, Mel Beeby! If I was to spit in your face, you'd go, 'Ooh Maia, I wonder why you did that? Is it maybe your tragic childhood?'"

I stared at her. I was getting an empty feeling behind my belly button that was a lot like feeling sick.

"I can read your mind, remember?" she warned. "You're thinking 'Lola would never speak to me like that'. 'Why isn't good lovely Lola here instead of bad evil Maia!'"

I flushed. "No, I'm not!" But that's exactly what I was thinking.

At that exact moment, Khamsin's kitty biffed her head forcefully against my hip pocket. That's what it felt like, though she couldn't *actually* have biffed me, she was visible and solid and I was in my angelic light body. Still, whatever it was that she did, I felt, or heard, a tiny clunk in my pocket.

I could not *believe* I'd forgotten about my mobile. I could have been calling Lola up for chats all this time!

Of course when I took the phone out, it turned out I'd brought Lola's by mistake. No probs. I could just call my own number.

I didn't mean to peek at Brice's text message. It flashed up all by itself.

no angel chick called maia known here,

tell mel b v. careful luv b

My whole Universe went blurry. I genuinely thought I was going to pass out.

"Who's your text from?" Maia's voice was so close, my heart almost jumped into my mouth.

I instantly pressed DELETE.

"Oh, it's not for me," I told her quickly.

I actually managed to smile, but my mind was racing, remembering Lola on the tour bus: *Has anyone but you actually seen this angel girl?*

And she never once came inside the hostel, I thought.

Maia wasn't an angel at all.

"If it wasn't for you, why do you look so upset?" she insisted.

You couldn't hide anything from Maia. I'd have to give her a reason she could relate to. "You bet I'm upset," I snapped. "Lola's gone off with my new phone and left me with her rubbish one." I coolly returned her stare.

Suddenly she broke into a grin. "Ooh, naughty naughty! If I didn't know you were an angel, I could have sworn I saw your Dark side then! OK, I'm off. I'll just be an hour or so. Sure you don't want to come?"

I shook my head, keeping my smile fixed in place until she vanished.

I almost collapsed on to the deck there and then, but I was scared she might be hanging around, checking up on me. I tottered below decks on jelly legs, desperately aiming to look casual.

The girls were still fast asleep.

I was so upset, I was literally gnawing at my nails, something I hadn't done for years. I couldn't believe that an hour ago I had wanted to save her. I felt so stupid. Stupid gullible Mel.

Khamsin and Amisi were starting to stir, giving each other sleepy smiles, like, "Hi, another perfect day on Cleopatra's barge."

If they only knew.

All day I was like a cat on a hot roof, waiting for Maia to pop up with her mad giggle, and wondering what the sassafras I'd say when she did. But hours went by and she still didn't show.

Somehow I held it together until the girls had gone to bed.

Then I went up on deck and started pacing and talking to myself like a seriously disturbed angel girl. I didn't know what to do. Was I just supposed to wait here like a fool till she finally decided to show up with some big made up story?

Khamsin's cat had followed me up on deck. She perched herself on the ornamental lotus on the prow, watching me closely, her eyes like tiny glowing moons in the dark, as I paced and muttered.

Maia the cosmic liar with her pants on fire. And I'd known from Day One. So I'd been lying to myself about Maia lying to me. I'd allowed her to blatantly run rings around me ever since that day at the museum.

"I can't just do nothing," I whimpered to myself.

The cat blinked her moonlit eyes.

That's right, you can't, babe, and you mustn't – that's giving her total control of the situation.

It was almost like Lola was there with me. That's so exactly what she'd say.

"But that means I'd have to go and find her?" I whispered.

I'm truly not good at confrontations.

I could hear the kitty's husky purr.

Don't think, babe, just do it, my soulmate said firmly inside my head.

Yeah, just do it, Mel, I told myself shakily.

I'd clocked up a lot of shimmering experience on my last mission, morphing through inner city

London like a pro – but then I'd known where I was going! Since I had no idea where Maia was, I focused on the little Hell minx herself and sent myself wherever.

SHIMMER.

The boat with its peaceful river sounds disappeared.

Drunken singing drifted from a scuzzy Egyptian bar. Even from outside you could tell it was a real dive.

She was sitting outside in the dirt with two other PODS teenagers. Between them they'd accumulated a large collection of empty bottles which I assume they'd brought with them.

The boy was got up like a crude look-alike of my buddy Reuben, down to the baby dreads, presumably a PODS idea of a joke. He gave off that type of Darkness you normally only meet in dreams.

I didn't waste my energy on the girl. One glance at that evil Lola clone was enough.

The boy sussed my vibes without looking up. "Oh-oh," he sniggered, "You've blown it now, Mazzie baby!"

"Yeah, *carita*," drawled the girl clone, taking off Lola's voice and failing big time. "Little Miss Innocent, she looks REALLY mad!!"

To my surprise, Maia went as white as a sheet. For once I'd done the last thing she expected.

She hissed something to her mates in a language that made my head hurt. There was a muddy ripple and suddenly they'd gone.

She jumped up, seeming genuinely agitated.

"Melanie, I know how this must look!"

I was shaking like a leaf, but I wasn't going to let her see.

"Let's see you charm your way out of this one, 'Mazzie baby'!" I told her.

Then Maia did the last thing *I* expected. She threw her arms around me, crying into my neck like a little kid.

"It's not like you think, Melanie! I *wanted* to come back to angel school, I really did," she wailed. "But those kids won't let me and now I'll have to stay in the Hell dimensions for ever!"

I had never knowingly been cried over by a PODS, and I was fairly sure it wasn't good for my health. I stealthily tried to prise myself free.

She took the hint and let me go. "I'm sorry I lied," she wept. "I never met Brice, but we all knew about him. He had a massive reputation at my school."

I bet! I could see him, slouching along in his ripped jeans, Hell fumes wafting from his Astral Garbage T-shirt.

"When you guys let him come back it rocked the whole school," Maia said tearfully. "A rumour started up that it was all down to this really special angel girl who had helped Brice straighten himself out." She darted a look under her lashes. "That was you, Melanie."

"Oh, don't insult me," I protested. "Even I'm not that stupid."

"No babe, listen," she said wiping her eyes. "I know Lola's been there for Brice, I do know that, but you're the one who really showed him he was on the wrong path. When he walked in on you and the little girl – Molly, wasn't it? – in the middle of that German air raid, you were so innocent and brave, you – you just blew him away." Maia's voice had gone husky with emotion.

She was saying something Lola often says herself. Of course that didn't mean it wasn't a trick. Plus as you can imagine I wasn't too thrilled at the idea of my name being thrown around the Hell dimensions.

"I want to go back home, Mel!" she wailed. "I want to wake up to the smell of wild lilacs, like when

I started angel school. But I took the wrong path like Brice." Tears and snot were getting mixed up on her face but Maia was so beside herself, she didn't seem to care. "I made a huge mistake," she sobbed. "Don't you think I KNOW that? That's why I need *you*, Melanie, to help me put it right!"

I was stunned. "Maia, I don't have that kind of power—"

"You DO! You just have to let me help you with some really big case!" she wept.

"Mission," I corrected.

She nodded humbly, wiping her nose with her sleeve. "I was thinking something like the saving Egypt thing," she said in a slightly calmer voice. "If I helped you pull that off, the Agency would have to see I'd changed, yeah? You said everyone deserves a second chance, right?"

As usual, Maia had totally spun me around. I wanted to believe her story about innocent Mel with the power to touch Dark angels' hearts. I wanted to be that incredibly special angel girl she described.

"So why didn't you tell me the truth right off?" I asked dubiously.

"That's what I keep asking *myself*," she wailed. "*Like, just tell her the truth, you silly mare! Mel can*

handle it! I guess lying is too much like second nature now." She blew her nose loudly – on a tissue I was relieved to see. "Sometimes I almost believe *myself*, you know?"

I felt a reluctant twinge of sympathy. Believing your own lies isn't totally exclusive to Dark angels. But too many things still weren't adding up.

"If you were so desperate to win yourself some brownie points with the Agency, why the sassafras didn't you support me and the girls when you had the chance?" I heard myself ask.

"I know!" Maia said earnestly. "I SO let you down, but Melanie, truly, I've been under the *most* stress. Those kids you saw just now used to be my mates, but when they heard about my plan to switch Agencies, they went totally Dark on me: harassing me twenty-four seven, sending horrible texts threatening to expose me." I saw her swallow hard. "Just before you showed up, they were saying I have to do this really evil dare or they'll—"

"Or they'll—?"

Maia gave a frightened whimper. "Don't. I'm scared, Mel. I know I've been into some bad stuff, but Leela and Rufio are in a league all by themselves."

Leela and Rufio. Even their names were creepy echoes of my angel buddies' names.

"One chance, that's all I'm asking! Just don't make me go back," she begged. "Please don't make me go back to that place."

I had a chilling flash of Sky walking off into the dark.

Now I ask myself: would I have acted differently if Helix had been there to guide me? But when you're all alone in the Universe, you sometimes have to take a risk and hope it will turn out for the best.

"One chance," I agreed huskily. "But no more games."

"I swear!" Maia promised, sniffing back her tears, and she gave me a sweet if wobbly smile.

"Omigosh," she said suddenly in a wondering voice. "I guess this is like the first day of the rest of my life, right? This is where I finally get a handle on all that love and light stuff?"

"Yeah," I said suddenly uneasy, "I guess it is."

And we shimmered back to Cleopatra's barge to begin Maia's new life.

Chapter Sixteen

"You know what I just realised?" I said to Maia one morning.

The barge was gliding past a typical Egyptian village, set among a patchwork of unnaturally bright green fields.

"Sorry babe, I was miles away. What?"

"These strips of land alongside the banks *are* basically Egypt! Like, ALL of it! The rest is just pure sand stretching on forever."

"Wow," Maia said in an interested voice. "I suppose that's right."

"I totally get now why Cleopatra admires those old-style pharaohs. They built that whole massive civilisation out of sand and river mud basically."

Like all the villages we'd seen, this one had a

water wheel, kept turning by a plodding donkey, to ensure the villagers' crops were well watered. In a country where it rains once in twenty years if you're lucky, water is unbelievably precious.

"It looks so permanent, doesn't it," I said wistfully.

You couldn't travel through Egypt in these times, and *not* know that the lives of ordinary Egyptians hung by a thread. Basically, everyone's survival depended on the yearly floods. If the Nile rose too high, like Adjo said happened soon after Cleopatra became queen, seeds just rotted in the earth, and everyone went hungry. One year the waters rose so high that the crocodiles swam right into the flooded houses and snatched human babies out of their cradles.

But if the flood waters failed to rise at the right time, or they didn't rise high enough again, Egypt went hungry. Since you never totally know what Mother Nature has up her sleeve, everyone just had to trust they'd be taken care of.

"I don't know how they bear it," I said, half to myself.

Maia went quiet, gazing over the orchards and fields, resting her chin on her hands. "I guess that's why they love their gods so much," she said at last. "They know they *can't* bear it, without, you know, divine help."

I was gobsmacked. Maia was turning over her new leaf so fast it literally made me dizzy. Less than two days had passed since I agreed to help her get back to Heaven, yet she was already thinking like a true angel.

And she had totally kept her promise. These days she took equal turns minding the girls. And when Khamsin went down with a bad tummy bug, Maia actually asked humbly if I'd remind her of the approved Agency technique for sending vibes! She said she'd hate to do it wrong and accidentally make Khamsin worse.

She still went walkabout most days, but she was usually back after an hour or two. She said her wanderings helped her to get her head together, and I chose to believe her.

But I felt like Khamsin's cat, with her tail-tip tensely twitching.

I didn't trust Maia, not deep down.

You'd always be wondering, is Maia for real? Maia said that first night.

I still didn't know the answer to that question. I just knew if I left her alone with the girls, I'd get a panicky urge to check up on her.

Once I rushed up on deck, with a terrible premonition that something had happened to

Khamsin. Maia explained later that Khamsin just had a momentary wobble; she was scared her mum only *thought* she'd recreated Nefertiti's magical blend.

But when I showed up, Maia was totally on it. She had an arm around each girl, murmuring encouragingly. Her expression was so calm and caring, she could have been an angel in a picture book.

I felt incredibly ashamed of my nasty suspicions, yet no matter how hard I tried, they never totally went away.

For some reason Khamsin was taking ages to recover from her bug, despite Maia and me taking turns to pump healing vibes into her every hour on the hour, not to mention the strong herbal potions Lady Iras prepared with her own hands.

Sometimes after I'd been beaming vibes Khamsin would actually seem to perk up. But next time it was my turn I'd find her feeling as bad as ever.

Maia pointed out that Khamsin had been through a lot in a very short time. "We shouldn't be surprised if she's having a reaction," she said calmly.

But it disturbed me to see feisty Khamsin losing more of her sparkle every day.

When Lady Iras gave the girls an exquisitely elegant hand-painted glass bottle to hold the finished fragrance, Khamsin hardly glanced at it. It was Amisi who carefully decanted the blend from its old humble container.

One hot golden afternoon we sailed past the partially ruined buildings of an abandoned city. I heard Lady Iras tell the girls that Queen Nefertiti and the Pharaoh Akhenaten originally had it built to be their new, v. grandiose, capital city. They had left their old city behind at around the same time they decided to ban Egypt's old religion and declare themselves sun gods. (Khaled did say they were a bit mad.)

After Nefertiti died – or was murdered, no one seemed too sure – the old-style priests angrily pulled most of their new-style city down, and tried to have Nefertiti's name obliterated from history for ever.

Khamsin seemed really down after she heard this. I know I was. We'd both been thinking of Nefertiti's perfume as a magic potion which would solve Egypt's problems at one stroke – or one sniff.

Well, it clearly hadn't solved Nefertiti's problems, I thought, as we gradually left those depressing ruins behind.

It dawned on me that the girls and I had all been living in a kind of beautiful daydream and pretending it was real. Khamsin and Amisi didn't have too much life experience, but I was an angel. I had no excuse. How exactly had I imagined that one little bottle of perfume could save Egypt forever?

At that moment, Khamsin turned white and crumpled to the deck. Amisi ran to her with a cry.

Lady Iras held smelling salts under Khamsin's nose, quickly bringing her out of her faint.

"Everything went so dark," Khamsin kept saying shakily.

Lady Iras laid her hand on Khamsin's forehead. "You have a very high fever," she exclaimed. "You must get out of this hot sun and rest."

Amisi helped Khamsin back to the cabin. "I will sponge your face," she said gently. "That will soon bring the fever down."

Khamsin looked at Amisi as if she didn't know who she was.

"I wish I hadn't brought you now," she burst out in a strange high voice. "You're always following me around like a stupid little puppy. Sometimes I feel like I can't breathe."

Amisi gasped and ran out of the cabin, staying away all the rest of the day.

Next day Khamsin didn't seem to remember the hurtful things she'd said, but I could see Amisi retreating into herself. Maybe she'd always thought their friendship was too good to be true.

That day we were due to pass Giza. Adjo and Baraka had promised to take the girls to see the pyramids – they'd been talking about it for days. But when it came to it, Khamsin felt too weak to leave the boat. Khamsin and Amisi just sat watching the famous skyline silently slide past, as if they were watching all their fabulous dreams for the future gradually float out of reach.

Next morning, I woke before it was light to hear wild drumming and hundreds of voices singing some kind of joyful song of praise.

I rushed up on deck to find Maia peering through the morning mists, looking distinctly spooked.

People were emerging from their cabins, having grabbed wraps or bed sheets to make themselves decent. Even Khamsin made it up on deck. Everyone wanted to know who was singing in the mist. Whoever they were, they *adored* Cleopatra! I heard her name being sung over and over, and something about her being a living goddess and ruling Egypt forever.

A gap suddenly opened in the mist as the first rays of light streamed down to Earth. Everyone gasped.

The river was crowded with small papyrus boats, so thickly decorated with flowers they literally looked like little floating gardens!

Each fragile paper boat carried several villagers. One carried three bony old priests and a golden statue of Hapy, the river god.

Baraka called out to them, wanting to know who they were and what they wanted. It turned out these were villagers Cleopatra had helped when their homes were flooded out, soon after she became queen. She had arranged for new houses to be built, set further back from the Nile, and ordered grain to be sent from the royal granaries, enough to feed everyone until next harvest.

Hearing rumours of a mysterious royal barge travelling down their stretch of the Nile, the grateful villagers had brought gifts of food, flowers and precious spices; they even brought handmade toys for Cleopatra's little boy.

The villagers poured on to the barge, still drumming and singing Cleopatra's praises. They slung a garland of fresh lotus blossoms around Mardian's neck (I know!) and threw handfuls of marigolds, jasmine and coloured rice as if they were at a wedding.

Everyone seemed to catch the party spirit! Baraka and Adjo produced musical instruments. The slaves brought extra platters of food and jugs of wine. Even the kitty joined in, chasing after grains of rice, and allowing the village children to pet her.

Khamsin and Amisi seemed as enchanted as everyone else, though Khamsin still had shadows like dark thumbprints under her eyes.

Mardian was smiling and nodding to the beat. Thanks to everyone's hard work, a growing caravan of carpet-makers, jewellers and whoever was slowly snaking along the edge of the desert towards Alexandria. Mardian was probably thinking it wouldn't hurt to let their hair down for a few hours.

I noticed one of the priests on the edge of the party he'd helped to create. Silent and frowning, he seemed to be watching something the wildly celebrating villagers couldn't see.

I moved in front of him, wondering what was making him look so disturbed. To my horror, he was looking straight at Maia.

She had her arm around Amisi. I heard her whisper softly. "Pick up the lotus flower, sweetie, that's it, pick it up and put it in Khamsin's hair, let her know you're her friend."

Maia's voice was so sweet and lulling, I was suddenly finding it hard to think.

The Universe went into slow motion as she raised her forefinger, sketching a strange symbol in the air.

The flower was no longer a flower. It was black and scuttling with a spiked tail like a cartoon devil. In front of my eyes, Maia had turned a lotus into a scorpion.

Like a sleepwalker, Amisi slowly stretched out her hand. She was maybe two centimetres from picking up the deadly creature, when Khamsin's cat made an urgent warbling sound in her throat and broke the spell.

Amisi gasped, seeing what she'd been about to do. Snatching off her sandal she flipped the scorpion into the river.

Her face had gone chalky with shock. Amisi had only inherited snake magic from her ancestors, I remembered, not scorpion magic.

"The dark gods wanted to play a trick on your friend," the priest told her in his thin old man's voice. "But I knew the little cat would protect you both."

I was hot with shame. The little cat was not supposed to protect them. That was my job. I'd promised Khamsin's dad I'd take care of her – and then I'd put her at risk again and again, all because I refused to listen to my own instincts.

I stormed over to Maia. My voice sounded like an angry stranger's. "You were never at angel school!" I accused her. "You've been with the Dark Powers from the start."

Maia let out her random giggle. "You took your time figuring that one out, babe! Definitely one up to the 'PODS', wouldn't you say!"

I could see the divine lightning burn shimmering on her neck. I knew how she got it now – and why.

"You stole that sacred ankh," I said clenching my fists.

"Not such a smart move as it turned out!" she admitted. "Your poxy Light gods ripped it off my neck. Said I was disrespecting their culture. Jeez!"

"Leave now," I told her in my new rough voice, "and I'll spare your life."

"You'll spare my WHAT?" Maia gave an outraged laugh. "Can you just hear yourself!"

"Just go," I told her.

I had a mental flash of the painting in our dorm: the white robed angel banishing the demon back to its evil domain. Everything seemed so straightforward in the painting. The angel looked like an angel. The demon was a normal warty-faced demon. There's no way you could have got them mixed up with each other. Maybe life was simpler then?

Without realising, I was copying the old-style angel's body language, pointing a trembly finger away from Cleopatra's boat and Khamsin and Amisi, away from this beautiful planet forever.

As avenging angels go, it has to be said I wasn't that impressive. I'd been wearing the same scuzzy combats since we were time-napped. But I was so absolutely hopping mad, that a real flash of lightning spurted from my fingertip, to our mutual surprise.

"OK, I *get* it," Maia said sulkily. "It was boring anyway, making out your disgusting vibes didn't make me want to puke. Jeez, didn't you once wonder why I couldn't take your company for more than ten minutes?"

The second lightning spurt was bigger and brighter, and came a *lot* closer to Maia's head, briefly setting fire to her hair.

Well, it's a waste of energy reasoning with PODS. They'll just keep on messing with your mind, persuading you right is wrong and day is night, exactly what Maia had been doing to me since we met.

"I told you to go," I repeated. "Unless you *want* me to finish you off?"

The last spark of light left her eyes. "You're not the boss of me," she spat. "It's not over till I say!"

"It's over for me," I told her.

I pointed my finger a third and final time.

A sizzling lightning bolt shot out like a burning arrow, but before it could hit her, the air gave a muddy ripple and she'd gone.

I don't know what that old-style angel in the painting did after he'd banished the Dark being. I sat down among the bruised flower petals and dirty rice and cried. I felt SO stupid and ashamed.

I was dimly aware of the villagers leaving the barge, still singing their Cleopatra song as they rowed back to their homes.

The girls had disappeared off to their cabin. Slaves started to sweep up the thick carpet of blossoms.

The little she-cat padded over, sniffed my face, decided I'd live, then got on with the more important business of batting a stray lotus flower around the deck. Now and then she'd glance my way, like, *She's not* still *crying about that cosmic low life?*

"You *knew* she was a bad apple," I sobbed. "And Lola knew. She knew from Day One, but I wouldn't listen. What was I *thinking*, kitty? I already *had* the most fabulous friend in the Universe!"

I wiped my eyes. "We should check on the girls."

Maia had been gone half an hour at most, yet the atmosphere in the cabin was as clear and sweet as a temple bell.

The fact that I noticed now told me just how badly the vibes on this boat had been going downhill. *Some angel you are*, I told myself miserably.

Amisi was helping Khamsin plait her hair. They were chatting quietly together as if they'd never quarrelled. Afterwards they got out their oils. Khamsin unstoppered Lady Iras' fancy bottle and they took turns to sniff. They closed their eyes in total rapture and so did I.

"Almost there," whispered Khamsin. "Mother says in her notes we have to add just one drop of this."

Amisi held her breath as Khamsin dripped exactly one transparent silvery green drop into their elegant new bottle.

The room went totally hushed. The exquisite hand-coloured glass made it impossible to see the slow journey of that teeny drop of flower oil, or the actual moment when its mysterious essence mingled invisibly with the blend. But I felt it. We all did. Nefertiti's perfume was finished at last.

"This is going to change Egypt's destiny," Khamsin said softly.

Amisi nodded solemnly. "I know. Your parents would be so proud."

She reverently replaced the stopper, as if she was sealing up an enchanted potion. Despite everything these girls had been through, they were still like wide-eyed five-year-olds who believed in magic. After that first night, they had never once asked – even amongst themselves – why Cleopatra needed them. They had totally gone with the flow, somehow trusting that they had a part to play in this Egyptian fairy tale.

Maia didn't touch them, I thought. *Not inside, where it matters.*

Now she'd gone back into the dark where she belonged.

I waited for the blissful feeling of relief that would make me know we were home and dry. But deep down I knew Maia wasn't going to give up that easily.

Chapter Seventeen

There was no sign of Maia for the rest of our journey.

By the time we reached the lake dock at Mareotis, twelve days after we set out, I felt ninety-nine per cent confident we had seen the last of her, yet somehow I couldn't totally relax my guard.

We sailed into the harbour as dozens of small fishing boats were arriving back from their morning run, their decks heaped with wriggling fish. Big merchant boats rode at anchor, their creaky timbers breathing out the vibes and smells of far-off lands.

Not counting Lady Iras, the only humans we'd seen in Cleopatra's Egypt were pure Egyptians with straight black hair and nut brown skin. Here in Alexandria, humans of all colours and nationalities yelled at each other in dozens of different languages as they unloaded cargoes from all over the ancient world.

At the quayside, several seriously spangly horse-drawn chariots were waiting to take the travellers to the palace. The girls and Lady Iras shared one chariot. I squeezed myself in invisibly beside Khamsin.

The kitty popped her head out of the basket, sniffing the sea air with interest as the chariot sped along the wide, almost empty roads at a stonking pace.

This was a very different Egypt, a vibey city of dazzling white buildings, fresh sea breezes and sparkling air. Lady Iras eagerly pointed out local landmarks: the *Museon* where scholars from all over the world came to study astronomy, science and mathematics; Alexandria's famous library that contained manuscripts dating back to the dawn of human civilisation; the tomb of the legendary warrior, Alexander, who had given his name to this beautiful Mediterranean city.

"If you look out to sea, you can just make out the lighthouse of Pharos – of course you really need to see it at night!" Lady Iras seemed excited to be back.

Khamsin and Amisi looked dazed and nervous. As they climbed the blinding white steps to the palace, with rows of stony faced guards on either side, they totally stopped talking.

The guards at the gates sprang aside to let us pass and we were inside the palace of Queen Cleopatra VII.

All at once, I felt light-headed with relief. I'd done what the gods wanted. I'd delivered the girls and Nefertiti's magical perfume safely to the queen, and it felt like now nothing could really go wrong.

We passed through massive doors studded with emeralds, our feet fairly floating across the gleaming floors of polished black marble.

Everywhere you looked, you saw layer on layer of gorgeousness: exotic rugs laid over marble, elaborate carved furniture draped in sumptuous silks, fabulous woven tapestries glittering with gold and silver thread, hanging from walls panelled in exotic scented wood.

Another lady in waiting, Lady Charmian, met them outside the queen's private sitting room, obviously delighted that everyone was safely back in Alexandria. Mardian and Lady Iras went in first to speak with the queen. At last Khamsin and Amisi were ushered in.

At the far end of a light airy room, glass doors opened into a garden. I could see dancing leaves in a hundred shades of green and a waterfall of the most perfect creamy white roses.

Sitting on a silk covered couch, with her legs tucked under her and thousands of gleaming black braids falling around her face, was Queen Cleopatra.

Two little slave boys gently wafted ostrich plumes to keep her cool, as she hooted with laughter at something Mardian had said.

Imagine your ideal big sister: funny, warm, and worldly wise, with totally brilliant taste in clothes, times it by ten – and you're still only half way to imagining Queen Cleopatra!

She wore a gown of sea-green silk so fine, it was more like mist than fabric. As I expected, her eyes were heavily made up with sooty black eyeliner and some type of old-style eye shadow which exactly picked up the misty green of her dress. I'd been picturing her loaded down with snake-headed bangles, gold amulets and whatever but she just had two breathtaking pearls like huge glimmering teardrops dangling from her ears.

I saw Cleopatra's wonderful eyes go wide with interest as Lady Iras shepherded in the terrified girls.

"I hear you have brought me a rare and precious gift?" she said in Egyptian. "It seems the gods have woven all our destinies together in a most magical way."

Khamsin started rummaging for the perfume in her basket.

The queen shook her head, and I heard the tiny seed pearls on her braids tinkle. "The gods have waited long centuries to bring us all together. I too prefer to delay my pleasures. Come!" She patted the couch. "Tell me about your journey."

The girls shot panicky glances at Lady Iras but she smiled to go ahead. They seated themselves shakily on either side of the queen. Amisi looked as if she might burst into tears.

OK, delaying your pleasures, but this is Nefertiti's legendary perfume we're talking about! I'd have been mad-keen to get the stopper out of that bottle, but this *très* unconventional queen went on calmly putting these two girls at their ease.

Gradually they lost that dazzled look and became more like their normal selves.

The queen said gently, "You have come a long way solely on trust. It's time you knew why I have asked for my people's help."

I felt like I'd waited quite a long time to find this out myself!

I already knew from Khaled and Maryam that Rome's new leaders had summoned Cleopatra to Tarsus to appear before Mark Antony, and that she had stubbornly decided to go to what every one else feared would be her certain death. And I knew she had formed a mysterious plan to save herself and her kingdom. Now we were finally going to hear this huge state secret from the queen's own lips!

"I am going to outfit a ship, the most fabulously luxurious ship the world has ever seen," she told the girls. "My ship will be filled with all the exotic treasures Romans associate with strange eastern lands: leopard skin rugs, priceless silks, furniture made from solid gold, pearls and rubies the size of duck eggs... The Romans expect me to grovel before them, begging for mercy!" I saw a flash of anger in those smoky kohl-rimmed eyes. "But I shall sail into Tarsus like a queen out of the Arabian Nights!"

Didn't I tell you I was almost right! *That's* why the queen needed all those chefs, perfume makers and whatever! She *was* going to throw a party, the most outrageously extravagant party in ancient history! A party intended by Cleopatra as a not so subtle message to the Romans. Like: "You can't crush me and you can't crush Egypt. This is just a glimpse of her ancient mystical power."

Amisi looked as if she thought she was dreaming, but I could tell Khamsin's quick mind was busy. "You would amaze the Romans even more if you sailed into Tarsus like a *goddess*," she suggested daringly.

Cleopatra gave a delighted laugh "A goddess! Did you have a particular goddess in mind?"

Khamsin's eyes sparkled. "The goddess of love!"

Cleopatra clapped her hands. "Oh yes!"

"And you should scent the sails with incense," Amisi joined in excitedly. "Then each puff of wind will waft the fragrance to – to the waiting Romans."

To Mark Antony, she meant.

"So much talking makes me thirsty," Cleopatra commented, reaching out a graceful arm for her goblet.

I felt something pass through the room. A shadow. A vibe.

She *is* wearing a snake bangle, I thought in surprise.

173

I turned cold. It wasn't a bangle. A living snake was wrapping its golden coils around Queen Cleopatra's slender upper arm.

I hurled myself across the room yelling "SNAKE!" It was a reflex. It wasn't likely any human would actually hear.

No human did. But Khamsin's kitty heard. Her fur stood up on end and she let out an ear-splitting yowl of warning.

The queen gasped and the little slave boys dropped their fans in terror as the snake flickered out its forked black tongue.

It was shy little Amisi who took control.

"Stay still," she told the little boys. "I won't let it hurt you, Your Majesty," she whispered to the queen. "Snake magic is in my blood."

She closed her eyes and half-sang, half-chanted a droning little song. To humans and angels the words were meaningless babble; to the snake it sounded like a beautiful love song. It flowed harmlessly on to the silk couch, pouring itself on to the floor, where it lay writhing its coils, obviously in a state of bliss.

Still chanting, Amisi draped the blissed-out snake calmly around her wrist and carried it out into the garden, where she set it free.

A drop of blood had welled up on Cleopatra's lip where she'd bitten it to make herself keep still. Her face was like grey chalk. Charmian and Iras rushed to her with smelling salts.

"That is how I will meet my death," she told them, trembling. "I have seen it in a dream."

I didn't stay to listen to Cleopatra's dream. I had a Dark angel to deal with. No prizes for guessing what Leela and Rufio had been daring Maia to do, though I doubted she'd needed much persuading.

I shimmered in and out of rooms and eventually found her in the queen's bedroom.

"Oh, that was *low*," I told her in a shaking voice.

Maia was wearing the red dress and leggings she'd worn the first day I met her. She pretended to be admiring the quaint cosmetic jars on the queen's dressing table.

"I know, but then I blew it," she pouted into the mirror. "It would have been SUCH a cool ending. Hurray, sweet innocent Melanie saved the world again – oh, no, wait, evil Hell minx Maia got there first – aarggghh!!!" Maia gave a hideously realistic impression of someone dying of snakebite.

"I was just saving everyone a lot of trouble," she added casually. "Like she said, a snake gets her in the end. Why drag it out, I say!"

"Why?" I could hardly hear my own voice.

"Because that's what she believes, babe. I thought you'd know how this stuff works by now!"

I shook my head. "I mean why did you do it? Pretending you wanted to come back to Heaven; trying to make me like you?"

She shrugged. "I'm your dark side, sweetie! That's what we Hell minxes do."

"But what *good* does it do – you – or anyone!"

She held up a finger. "Can I give you a tiny tip, babe?" she said brightly. "Despite what your teachers tell you, things don't always have to make sense. I had a blast, OK?" Maia let out the daffy giggle she'd stolen from me. "Jeez, Louise! When you're rattling round a big empty Universe like a pointless cosmic pinball, you've got to get your laughs *somehow*!"

"So none of it actually had a point? You did it because you could, basically?"

Maia bounced on to the queen's enormous bed, giving me a sly little smirk. "You know what *really* upsets you? The way I can always read you! All those maggoty little secrets you try so pathetically hard to hide, are an open book to me. Being jealous of your best *friend*, Melanie! How sad is that?"

My face was burning. This was worse than that dream where you turn up to school in your underwear.

"You know what you are, babe?" she asked sweetly.

I felt unbelievably tired. "You tell me," I said wearily. "You've obviously got me all sussed."

"Allrighty," she said, giving another perky little bounce. "You, Mel Beeby, are a common little nobody who desperately longs to be somebody. You want everyone to say, 'Wow, I can hardly believe Mel grew up on that dodgy London estate! It's like she was totally *born* to be an angel!'"

"I don't think—"

"Exactly!" Maia pounced gleefully. "You don't *think*, full stop ! You *knew* I was bad news. You SAW me with my mates! You could have ended it then, but you let me con you into taking me back. Why? Because you thought it would make you look super-special when you got back to Heaven. Like, 'Oh, did you hear how Mel rescued that Dark angel girl from a life of eternal evil. She was hanging out with some real cosmic scum, but Melanie just refused to give up on her until finally she tamed her through the Power of Lurve!'"

Maia fell back on to the royal bed, laughing.

Every true dig she got in made me feel like I was losing a crucial layer of skin. There was no reason to think she wouldn't go on peeling away my layers for sheer enjoyment, the way mean little boys pull wings off flies.

There was only one way to make her stop. *I* had to do the peeling. I had to tell the truth – to Maia and to myself. The uncut, totally humiliating truth.

"You're right," I said shakily. "I did want to tame you with the Power of Lurve." I surprised myself with a yelp of amazed laughter. "How sad was I? As if you can save someone who doesn't want to be saved!"

Maia sat up, suddenly suspicious. "What's your game, Mel Beeby?"

I shook my head. "I'm not the one who plays games. I leave that to you, sweetie. Where was I? Oh, back to what you said about me being jealous of Lola. You were bang on target there too."

"Hey!" Maia made a fist. "Don't think you can try any funny business, OK?"

"Oh, this is SO not funny," I told her. "It's sad, exactly like you said. Lola is the best friend anyone could ever have, yet I've always been secretly jealous of her. Maybe I really wanted to *be* her. She's so talented. She's cool, she's confident. She could have any angel boy she wants, yet she's one hundred per cent faithful to Brice. Omigosh, I had such hideous thoughts. Some days I couldn't stand myself. But the more I tried to hide them..."

There was more, a lot more.

All those thoughts I'd imagined were so ugly and shameful but which just sounded – well, pathetic, actually – now I was hearing myself say them out loud. It was such a huge relief to let them go, like taking off a pair of super-tight hipsters you've technically outgrown yonks ago.

Maia seemed increasingly dazed, as I went on revealing all my bad deeds one after another, and my equally bad thoughts. She could not figure out *where* this was going.

Which made two of us. I just knew I was doing what I had to do. Finally I took a breath. "My turn."

She scowled. "Your turn to do what?"

Maia never did like surprises, unless she was in charge of the surprising.

I gave her a cool smile. "Well, you see, I'm just wondering, babe, when you get back to Hell school, if you'll be rushing to tell 'Leela' and 'Rufio', *your* maggoty little secrets? Like, all the time you were pretending you were my friend, a tiny part of you wanted it to be true."

Maia jumped off the bed. "Don't even go there!" she warned.

"Admit it!" I challenged her. "Isn't there a teeny speck of divine Light inside you that absolutely *longs* to go to my school and hang out with my friends and yes, wake up smelling lilacs. The same part which longs to let the hate go forever, so you can let in the lo—"

"Don't you *dare*!" Maia was literally blocking her ears. "Don't you EVER say that L-word to me!"

"Sorry, babe, it's a cosmic law. If you're my Dark side, obviously I have to be your Light side!"

As I said it, I knew it was true.

"Oh, and another thing!" I remembered. "You're supposed to be my worst nightmare, yeah? Did you ever stop to wonder what happens to the evil Hell minx when the innocent angel girl wakes up from her bad dream?"

Maia opened her mouth and shut it again.

"Because I'm awake now, Maia! WIDE awake. I owe you for that. I mean it."

I was probably supposed to banish her now, like in that painting, but Maia and I come from a different generation. We have our own style of doing things. So I just walked away.

I noticed Khamsin's kitty pattering beside me and wondered how long she'd been there.

Don't think I wasn't scared. I'd seen what Maia could do, don't forget: turning lotus flowers to scorpions, making you think day was night. But I kept walking, refusing to even give her the satisfaction of turning round to see what she did next.

Nothing.

No frogs raining from the ceiling, no PODS tricks at all: just a sweet lovely vibe flowing through the palace, as the Dark energy that had pretended to be Maia was sucked back into its own dimension.

Maia had banished herself.

That's how I knew she was gone. Forever, I hoped, this time.

In the garden, Cleopatra's little boy was galloping over the grass pretending to be a chariot driver.

I could see them all through the open doors in the golden glow of late afternoon, framed by dancing leaves.

Seeming totally recovered from her shock, Cleopatra was making everyone sniff the insides of her wrists. Queen Nefertiti's perfume was obviously a hit!

"Notice how it changes with the warmth of my skin?" she told her attendants eagerly. "It's so fresh, like a summer dawn in my garden here in Alexandria. But underneath there is something most mysterious and intriguing!"

That'll be the costus, I thought, grinning to myself.

"Charmian, have the blue chamber prepared for our honoured guests!" Cleopatra commanded her lady in waiting. She put an arm around each of the girls' shoulders. "You will stay in my palace tonight," she smiled. "Tomorrow I want to hear all your ideas for turning my ship into Aphrodite's barque."

That's when I knew Khamsin was truly home and dry, in this life anyway.

I blew them all angel kisses, then turned to go.

A servant with a lighted taper was going from room to room lighting the lamps. It would soon be evening.

I wanted to fix it all in my mind for ever; the lovely light, the sea breezes which set the tapestries shivering and the lamps flickering, this palace which seemed as thrillingly alive as Cleopatra herself.

I heard a husky mew. Khamsin's cat was winding around my legs.

"No, kitty," I said softly. "You can't go where I'm going."

She gave an irritated squawk, like, *I'm the all-seeing eyes of Isis OK? I choose where I go, thank you VERY much!*

So the determined little kitty and I ended up going back through the long hall together, over the slippery black marble floor, past Cleopatra's guards, out through the barred gate, and down the steps, until we'd reached the street.

The kitty kept running in front of me, almost like she wanted to trip me up. She seemed v. stressed about something, like, *Will you just look at me, Melanie! No I mean REALLY look at me!!*

Suddenly I was crouching on the blistering hot pavement, gazing into a pair of intense moonlit eyes. I mentally replayed my exit from Cleopatra's palace. "Did you just *shimmer* through those gates, kitty?" I breathed.

"Oh, *finally*!" said Lola's voice inside my head.

I gasped. "Lollie? Is that really you in there?"

I felt a weird disturbance in the air.

We both looked up in time to see a shimmery white shape racing towards the palace steps at warp speed. Five seconds before it drew level, I recognised Maryam's jeep.

My tutors were in the front, looking like they drove to Cleopatra's times every day of the week.

"You weren't planning to *walk* into the future were you?" teased Khaled.

The kitty and I climbed in. Khaled put the jeep in gear and I felt my hair stream back as we blasted back to the twenty-first century.

"Doesn't she know how to turn back!" Maryam asked, amused.

"Actually, I'm not too—"

The little she-cat picked that moment to morph back into an irate Lola. "I can't believe you didn't recognise me, you pig!"

"Maybe because I wasn't expecting you to be wearing FUR!"

"What was I supposed to do?" Lola shot back. "When I lost you in the middle of that cosmic battle, I was just screaming, 'I can't leave Mel, someone help me!'" Next minute I was floating down to Cleopatra's times! So I guess someone helped."

Someone like the gods, I thought, breaking into goose bumps.

Suddenly Lola was almost in tears. "Michael said I had to stick to you like glue. I had this idea to turn myself into a cat so I could look after you without Maia knowing. Sorry, trainees aren't really supposed to shape-shift unless it's a cosmic emergency," she added hushly with a worried glance at our tutors.

"Oh, that *definitely* counted as a cosmic emergency," Khaled said a little grimly.

Then Lola and I just hugged each other and cried.

CHAPTER EIGHTEEN

Before we left Egypt, Khaled and Maryam organised a private celebration for us at Maia's magical Nile cafe.

When we rocked up, I was amazed to see Michael chatting to our tutors.

He was obviously delighted to see me and Lola safe and sound. He poured out sparkling pomegranate juice for us all, and everyone congratulated me all over again on getting through the Test with flying colours. I'd even had a text from Brice telling me well done!

I'd survived an ordeal I never knew existed.

Instead of feeling proud, I just felt confused – and, well, *betrayed*. How could a divine Agency turn a deranged angel girl loose in a dangerous Universe, with just her inner fruitcake for guidance?

Also, if I'd truly passed – durn durn durn – THE TEST, and come safely out the other side to popping champagne corks, like everyone was making out, why didn't Helix come back? Now my cosmic crazies had worn off, I was aware of a kind of foggy void where my divine guidance system ought to be.

No one seemed able to tell me if this was, like, a temporary after effect of the Test, and if so how long this phase would last.

But Michael had taken time out from a hectic cosmic schedule to toast my achievement, so I swallowed down all my questions and tried to make an effort.

Our headmaster listened patiently as Lola and I babbled two versions of our big Nile adventure simultaneously, from our two legged and four legged perspectives.

About half way through, we had an interesting discussion about why I didn't get sick on the boat despite spending so much time with the high-school girl from Hell. Michael thought it was because the Light coming from all the humans on the boat, Mardian, Lady Iras and whoever, was simply too strong. It was Maia who got sick, as she'd so charmingly pointed out. Khamsin got sick too, of course, but only because Maia deliberately plugged her full of toxic vibes.

Then we went back to describing Cleopatra's palace, and of course young charismatic Queen Cleopatra herself.

"I wish Maia hadn't told me about her dying of snake bite," I said wistfully.

I wanted to remember Cleopatra putting her arm round Khamsin and Amisi going, "Charmian, have the blue chamber prepared for our honoured guests!"

I literally jumped up spilling my juice. *Golden shoes.*

"Michael, I just realised! Sky – well, really Khamsin – got to sleep over in Cleopatra's palace for real!"

"Oh she did much better than that," he said mildly.

He opened up his shimmery white laptop and suddenly we were watching cosmic footage of Cleopatra's treasure ship.

"Omigosh, can you believe that hussy went for *purple* sails!" Lola shrieked.

Like a modern-day celeb, Queen Cleopatra knew exactly how to promote herself, picking the perfect time of day to sail into Tarsus, so she'd be sailing right into the setting sun. The slaves' silver-tipped oars shimmered and flashed, making it seem as if this magical ship was giving off its own divine light.

Michael zoomed in, and Lola and I *oohed* and *aahed* to see Cleopatra draped over a leopard-skin couch in a frankly cheesy goddess pose. She was dressed in pure gold from head to toe, making it seem like she'd just that minute flown down from a starry Heaven. She was showing a LOT of cleavage I have to say!

Lady Iras and Lady Charmian reclined adoringly at her feet, dressed as sea nymphs. The two younger sea nymphs beside them seemed strangely familiar. My heart gave a delighted skip as I recognised Khamsin and Amisi giving it all they'd got!

Now we were zooming in on a burly Roman in military uniform, waiting on the dock with his awe-struck lieutenants.

"Look at Mark Antony's face!" breathed Lola. "He thinks he's dreaming!"

"Wait till he smells Nefertiti's perfume," I giggled.

It's a strange feeling, knowing you're one tiny part of an awesome pattern woven by gods and angels, runaway perfume makers, divine cats and incredibly cunning and resourceful queens.

If one tiny element had been changed, if I never knew Sky, if my inner fruitcake hadn't made me rush off to Egypt to save the world, if Khamsin hadn't run out to buy apricots, if Amisi had been born without the snake magic in her DNA – would Cleopatra's meeting with Mark Antony still be remembered thousands of years later as one of the most romantic moments in human history?

I was only sure of one thing. Khamsin would never have made it to Cleopatra's court alive without a determined tufty-eared kitty.

I wasn't alone, I realised, and I started to smile to myself, *I had my faithful inner kitty to take care of me!*

"I knew you'd send her packing in the end," Lola told me softly.

"How could you know?" I asked amazed. "I was being such a total idiot."

My soulmate squeezed my hand and repeated with total confidence, "I knew, *carita*, OK? I just knew."

*Answer: None. If the angel is doing her job properly, the light bulb will v-e-r-y slowly and gradually change itself!

Don't miss the amazing mission that started it all...

TIME: My 13th Birthday

PLACE: Heaven

MISSION: Enrol at angel school!

REPORT: One minute I'm crossing the road, working out the clothes I'm going to buy with my birthday money, then – BANG! – I'm a student in some posh angel school, learning about halos. At least the uniforms are cool...

www.agentangel.co.uk